MOTOR BOAT BOYS ON THE GREAT LAKES

BY

LOUIS ARUNDEL

Motor Boat Boys On The Great Lakes

CHAPTER I

UP A TREE

"What a funny cow that is, Josh! Look at the silly thing poking her bally old horns in the ground, and throwing the dirt up. Say, did you ever see anything like that? Why, the poor beast must be sick, Josh!"

"Cow? Great Jupiter! Buster, you silly, don't you know a bull when you see one?"

"Oh, dear! and just think of me having the nerve to put on my nice red sweater this morning, because this Michigan air was so nippy. I don't believe bulls like red things, do they, Josh?"

"They sure don't. And then we had to cut across this field here, to save a few steps. He's looking at us right now; we'll have to run for it, Buster!"

The fat boy, who seemed to fully merit this name, set down the bucket of fresh milk he had been carrying, and groaned dismally.

"I just can't run—never was built for a sprinter, and you know it, Josh Purdue!" he exclaimed. "If he comes after us, I've got to climb up this lone tree, and wait till he gets tired."

"Then start shinning up right away, Buster; for there he comes—and here I go!"

With these words long-legged Josh started off at a tremendous pace, aiming for the nearest fence. Buster, left to himself, immediately commenced to try to get up the tree. He was so nervous with the trampling of the bull, together with the hoarse bellow that reached his ears, that in all probability he might have been caught before gaining a point of safety, only that the animal stopped once or twice to throw up some more soil, and thus give vent to his anger at the intrusion on his preserves.

Josh got over the ground at an amazing rate, and reaching the fence proceeded to climb over the topmost rails; never once relinquishing his grip on the package of fresh eggs that had just been purchased from the farmhouse, to make a delicious omelette for a camp dinner.

Meanwhile, after a tremendous amount of puffing, and frantic climbing, the fat boy had succeeded in getting a hold upon the lower limb, and pulled himself out of the danger zone just as the bull collided with the trunk of the tree.

"Gosh!" exclaimed Buster, as he hugged his limb desperately; "what an awful smash that was! And hang the luck, he's just put his foot in our pail of milk too. There goes the shiny tin bucket the farmer loaned me, flying over the top of the tree, I guess."

He presently managed to swing himself around so that he could sit upon the limb and look down at his tormentor. The bull was further amusing himself by tearing up a whole lot more of the turf, and bellowing furiously.

"Mad just because you didn't get me, ain't you, mister?" mocked Buster; whose name was really Nick Longfellow, strange to say, considering how short and stout nature had made him.

The bull did not bother answering, so after watching his antics for a minute, and wondering if he, too, would have been tossed over the tree had he been caught, Nick remembered that he had had a companion in misery.

Upon looking across the field he saw Josh perched on the rail fence, surveying the situation, craning his long neck to better observe the movements of the animal, and ready to promptly drop to the ground at the first sign of danger.

"Hey, Josh! ain't you goin' to help a feller?" shouted the prisoner of the lone tree in the pasture.

"Course I'd like to, Buster; but tell me, what can I do?" answered the other. "Perhaps now you'd like to have me step inside, and let the old thing chase me around, while you scuttled for the fence. What d'ye take me for, a Spanish bull-baiter? Well, I ain't quite so green as I look, let me tell you."

"That's right, Josh," replied the fat boy with emphasis; "and it's lucky you ain't, 'cause the cows'd grabbed you long ago for a bunch of juicy grass. But why don't you do something to help a feller out of a hole?"

"Tell me what I can do, and I'll think about it, Buster," answered the other; as though not wholly relishing the remark of his comrade, and half tempted to go on his way, leaving the luckless one to his fate.

"If you only had my red sweater now, Josh, you might toll the old feller to the fence, and keep him running up and down while I slipped away."

"Well, send it over to me then," replied the tall boy, with a wide grin.

"You just know I can't," declared the prisoner. "Don't I wish I had wings right now; or somebody'd drop down in an aeroplane, and snatch me out of this pickle? But I suppose I'll have to get up a way of escape myself. Don't I want to kick myself now for not thinking about a packet of red pepper when

I was at that country store down near Pinconning yesterday. Never going to be without it after this, you hear, Josh?"

Only recently Nick had read an account of how a boy, on being hard pressed by a pack of several hungry wolves, somewhere in the north, had shown remarkable presence of mind in taking to a tree, and then scattering cayenne pepper in the noses and eyes of the fierce brutes as they jumped up at his dangling feet.

In that case the brutes had gone nearly crazy with the pain, and the boy easily made his way home. The story had impressed Buster greatly, and that was why he now lamented the fact that he had no such splendid ammunition to use on the bull.

"Say, suppose you toss down that red sweater to him," suggested Josh, making a speaking trumpet of both his hands.

"What good would that do?" demanded the captive, plaintively; for he was unusually fond of the garment in question, and gloried in wearing it; though after this experience he would be careful about how he donned it again while ashore.

"Oh! he might take to tossing it around, and perhaps run to the other side of the field. Then you could sneak for the fence," called the one who was safe.

"Yes, and have him come tearing after me before I was half way there," cried Nick. "I guess not. Think of something easier. Can't you coax him over there, Josh? Oh! please do. I half believe you're as much afraid of him as I am."

"Who says I am?" retorted the other, at once boldly jumping down inside the fence; upon which the bull started on a gallop for that quarter, and it was ludicrous to see how the valiant boaster went up over that barricade again, sprawling flat as he jumped to the ground.

Nick laughed aloud.

"He near got you that time, Josh!" he cried. "Ain't he the terror though? Look at him smash at that fence. Better keep an eye out for a tree, I tell you, if he breaks through. And Josh, for goodness sake save the eggs. Our milk is gone, the tin pail is ruined; but we don't want to lose the precious eggs."

A few seconds later Nick broke out into a loud wail.

"Hold on, Josh," he called; "I was only fooling when I said that about you being afraid. Of course you ain't; only it stands to reason nobody wants to let that old bull get a chance to lift him with those horns. Don't go away and leave your best chum this way, Josh."

"Chuck it, Buster," called back the other. "I'm not going to desert you. But somebody's got to go after the farmer, and get him to come and coax the bull to be good. You can't go, so I'm the only one left to do the job. Hold on tight, and don't talk the bull to death while I'm gone."

"Oh! bless you, Josh!" called the captive of the tree. "I always knew you had a big heart. But don't be too long, will you; because if he keeps banging the trunk of this rotten old tree all the time and chipping off pieces, I'm afraid he'll get it down yet. Hurry, now, Josh! Tell the farmer what a mess I'm in; and that he's just got to bring out some feed, and coax his mountain of beef to be good. Hurry, please, Josh, hurry!"

He watched the tall boy making his way leisurely along, and groaned because Josh seemed determined to let him have quite a siege of it there.

The bull had come back, and was nipping the grass almost under the tree. Now and then he would move off a little distance, and deliberately turn his back on Nick, as though he had forgotten that such a thing as a boy existed. But the captive was not so easily deceived.

"No you don't Mr. Bull!" he called, derisively. "I can just see you looking this way out of the corner of your eye. Like me to slip down, and try to make that old fence, wouldn't you? Guess I'd sail over the rails with ten feet to spare. But think what an awful splash there'd be when I landed. I can wait a while, till Josh takes a notion to tell what he came back for."

Minutes passed, and he grew more and more nervous. Long ago had his tall chum passed out of sight behind the clump of trees that shut off all view of the farmhouse. Nick half suspected that Josh was lying down somewhere, resting, perhaps in a place where he could watch what went on in the pasture.

"Oh! don't I wish I had wings now?" he kept mumbling, as he shook his head angrily, and watched the movements of the bull. "I'd fly away, and let Josh think the ugly old beast had swallowed me, that's what. He'd be sorry then he loafed, when I sent him for help. But is that him coming over yonder?"

He thought he had detected something moving; but it was at a point far removed from the place where he expected Josh and assistance to show up.

"Well, I declare, if it ain't George!" he exclaimed presently. "He must have begun to believe we were having too good a time at the farmhouse; and is on his way over to get his share. George is always looking for a pretty girl. I've got half a notion to let him get part way across the field, and then holler at him. When a feller is in a scrape it makes him feel better to see somebody else getting it in the neck too. There he comes across, sure enough!"

The bull had evidently seen George, too; but as he happened to be standing half concealed by the trunk of the tree just then, the boy who so lightly started to cut across the pasture, meaning to head for the house among the trees, failed to discover the bull.

"Oh! my, won't he be surprised though!" muttered Nick, craning his fat neck in order to see the better; for he did not want his friend to get so far along that, in a pressure, he could not gain the fence before the coming of the wild bull.

Now the beast had started to paw the ground. George stopped short as he caught the sound, and looked around him. Just then the bull tore up some more turf, and tossed it in the air. That meant he was primed to start on a furious rush to overtake the newcomer.

"Run, George!" shrieked the boy in the tree, at the top of his high-pitched voice. "Run for the fence! He's got his eye on you! The bull's coming like hot cakes! Go it for all you're worth, George. Oh! my! did I ever see such a great lot of sprinting! George can run pretty near as good as Josh did, and that's saying a heap."

It was. George seemed to be making remarkably fine time as he shot for that friendly fence. Evidently George knew something about bulls; enough at least not to want to stay in an enclosure with an angry one, and interview him.

For a very brief period of time it seemed nip and tuck as to whether George would be allowed to get over that barrier unassisted, or be helped by the willing bull. But apparently, after one look over his shoulder at the approaching cyclone, George was influenced to let out another link, for his speed increased; and he just managed to scramble over the rails when the bull came up short against the fence, to look through with his red eyes, and shake his head savagely.

"Hey! where are you, Buster?" shouted George, after he had succeeded in getting his breath again.

"Here, in this bally old tree, George. He chased us, and I had to hustle up here, while Josh went for help. He knocked my milkpail to flinders; but thank goodness Josh saved the eggs!" cried Nick; whose greatest failing was a tremendous appetite, that kept him almost constantly thinking of something to eat.

"Say, you're a nice one," called the other. "Why didn't you warn me sooner?"

"I'm real sorry now I didn't, George," replied Nick, as if penitent; though at the time he was shaking with laughter, just as a bowl of jelly quivers on being moved; "but I was in hopes you'd scare him off. When I saw him getting mad, I knew he had it in for you; and then I yelled. But George, please think of some way to coax the old rascal off, won't you. It's awful hard on me sitting up here on this limb, and he means to stay till I just starve to death. Have pity on me George and get up some plan to rescue your best chum."

CHAPTER II

THE CAMP IN THE COVE

"Hey, Buster," cried the one on the other side of the fence, "where did you say Josh was?"

"He went for help, over to the farmhouse where we got the milk and eggs," answered the boy in the tree.

"Well," George went on, after looking all around. "I don't see him coming any too fast; and I wouldn't put it past that joker to take a snooze on the way, so as to make you worry a lot more."

"Yes, I was just thinking that same thing myself, George. Josh has got it in for me, you know, every time. But please think up some way to toll this angry gentleman cow away, George."

"If I only had that red sweater now, I believe it could be done," said George, presently.

"Why, that was what Josh said too," lamented the prisoner; "but don't you see I can't get it over to you at all?"

"Course not; but hold on there!" called George.

"Oh! now I know you've thought of an idea. Good for you, George! You're the best friend a fellow ever had, when he was in trouble. Are you going to sneak in the pasture, and tempt the bull away?"

"I am not," promptly responded George. "I've got too much use for my legs, to take the chances of being crippled. But wait and see what I'm going to do. Trust your Dutch uncle to fool that old cyclone. Look at him tossing the dirt up again. Oh! ain't he anxious to get at me, though?"

"What's that you're shaking at him now?" demanded Nick. "It looks like my sweater, only I know yours is gray. Why, it must be a bandanna handkerchief; yes, I remember now, you often tie one around your neck, cowboy fashion. I can see that you're going to get me out of this nasty fix, George. It takes a lawyer sometimes to beat a bull at his own game."

"It is a bandanna, Buster," replied the other, "and watch me coax the old fellow along the fence, down to the other end of the field. How he shakes his head every time I wave the red flag, and tries to get at me. It's working fine, Buster. You get ready to drop down and run when I tell you."

"But George, even if you coax him to the end of the pasture you know I'm so slow I never could make the fence before he caught up with me?" cried the still worried prisoner of the tree.

"Yes, you are like an ice wagon, Buster; but never mind. I've got all that fixed. Just look down yonder and you'll see a nice little trap ready for Mr. Bull. It's a small enclosure, with three long rails to slide across, once he's inside. Then he's caught fast, and can't get out. That is meant for just such a purpose. See?"

"Bully! bully!" shouted the delighted Nick, waving his hat in the air. "Oh! I tell you it takes a smart fellow to get on to these dodges. Why, Josh must have been blind not to see that same thing. Look at the bull following you every time you take a step. Then he turns his old head to peek back at me, as if just daring me to try and make the fence. But I know better. I can wait. Why, George, talk to me about your Spanish bull fights, this sure takes the cake!"

"Don't crow too soon," answered the other boy. "Now comes the ticklish part of the game. Will he go in that enclosure, or balk?"

"Wave it harder, George! Make out that you're going to climb over. That's the way to hold him. My! but wouldn't he like to pitch you higher'n a kite. Look at that piece of old fence rail go flying, would you? Now he's inside, George! Oh! if you can only get the bars across!"

George proved equal to the emergency. He fastened his red handkerchief to the fence, so that the wind kept it stirring constantly, with the bull snorting just on the other side, and smelling of the flaming object. Then George slily slipped back, took hold of the upper bar, and quickly shot it in place through the opposite groove.

A second immediately followed; and by the time Mr. Bull awakened to the fact that he had again fallen into the old trap, he found himself neatly caged.

Nick was wild with delight. Still talking aloud, partly to himself and also addressing fulsome remarks to his chum, he started to slide down the body of the tree, landing with a heavy thump on the ground.

Then he went off at a pretty good pace, for one so stout, heading for the nearest part of the friendly fence.

Just about this moment, when Nick was half way across the intervening space, who should appear but Josh, followed by a farmer bearing a measure of corn as a lure intended to entrap the fighting animal.

All Josh saw was his friend trotting over the field; and filled with sudden alarm lest poor Nick be overtaken by the wily bull, whom he supposed to be on the other side of the tree, he immediately broke out into a shrill shout.

"Run faster, Buster! He'll sure get you! Put on another speed! Hurry, hurry!"

When the fat boy heard these wild cries he became visibly excited. It was all very well to tell him to gallop along at a livelier clip; but Nature had never intended Nick Longfellow for a sprinter. When in his new alarm he attempted to increase his speed, the consequence was that his stout legs seemed to get twisted, or in each other's way; at any rate he took a header, and ploughed up the earth with his stubby nose.

It gave him a chance to roll over several times, as if avoiding a vicious lunge from the wicked horns of the bull, which animal he imagined must be closing in on him.

Struggling to his feet, he again put for the now near fence; and George nearly took a fit laughing to see the remarkable manner in which the fat boy managed to clamber over the rails, heedless of whether he landed on his feet or his head, so long as he avoided punishment.

When Josh came running down, accompanied by George, Nick was brushing himself off, and wheezing heavily.

"Give you my word, Buster," said the long-legged boy, penitently, "I never saw that the old duffer was caught in that trap when I yelled. Thought he was only hiding behind the tree, and giving you a fair start before he galloped after. George, did you do that smart trick? Well, it never came to me, I give you my word. Everybody can't have these bright ideas, you know. And Nick, I was bringing the farmer, with a measure of corn, to get the bull to the barn. Hope you don't hold it against me because I yelled. I sure was scared when I saw you trotting along so easy like."

Nick was of a forgiving nature, and could not hold resentment long.

"Oh! that's all right, Josh," he said. "No great harm done, even if I have torn a big hole in my trouser knee. But you stayed away a mighty long while. Seemed like a whole hour to me."

"Oh!" replied Josh, with a twinkle in his eye, "not near as long as that. Course it seemed like it to you, because a feller in a tree is worried. I had some trouble finding the farmer, you know. But let's go back and get some more milk. Here's my eggs all sound. Never broke one, even when I piled over this fence in such a hurry."

The rest were of the same mind; so, accompanied by the amused Michigan farmer, they walked back to the house, where another purchase was made. Not only did they get milk, and another pail; but George thought to ask about butter, and secured a supply for camp use.

This time they avoided all short-cuts as tending to breed danger.

"I've heard said that 'the longest way around is the shortest way to the fire,'" laughed George, as they passed the trapped bull; "but I never knew it applied to cow pastures as well. Just remember that, will you, Buster?"

"Just as if I could ever forget those wicked looking horns," answered the fat boy promptly. "I guess I'll dream about that bull often. If you hear me whooping out in the middle of the night, boys, you can understand that he's been chasing me in my sleep. Ugh! forget him—never!"

In about ten minutes they came out of a grove of trees, and before them lay the great lake called Huron. Although it was something of a cove in which a campfire was burning, beyond, as far as the eye could reach, stretched a vast expanse of water, glittering in the westering sun, for it was late in the afternoon at the time.

Three natty little motor boats were anchored in the broad cove, back of a jutting tongue of land that would afford them shelter should a blow spring up during the night from the northeast, something hardly probable during early August.

Near the fire a trio of other lads were taking things comfortably. One of these was Jack Stormways, the skipper of the Tramp; another Jimmie Brannagan, an Irish lad who lived in the Stormways home on the Upper Mississippi, as a ward of Jack's father, and who was as humorous and droll as any red-haired and freckled face boy on earth; while the third fellow was Herbert Dickson, whose broad-beamed boat was called the Comfort, and well named at that.

George Rollins commanded the slender and cranky speed boat which rejoiced in the name of Wireless, and Josh acted as his assistant and cook; while Nick played the same part, as well as his fat build would allow, in the big launch.

They had spent a month cruising about the Thousand Islands, where fortune had thrown them in the way of many interesting experiences that have been related in a previous volume. Just now they were making a tour of the Great Lakes, intending to pass up through the famous Soo canal, reach Lake Superior, knock around for a few weeks, and then head for Milwaukee; where the boats would be shipped by railroad across the country to their home town on the great river.

As soon as the three wanderers arrived, laden with good things, Josh, who was the boss cook of the crowd, began to start operations looking to a jolly supper on the shore.

There were a few cottages on the other side of the little bay; but just around them it was given over to woods, so that they need not fear interruption during their evening meal, and the singing feast that generally followed.

Out in the bay a large power boat was anchored, a beautiful craft, which the boys had been admiring through their marine glasses. Possibly the flutter of girls' white dresses and colored ribbons may have had something to do with their interest in the costly vessel, though neither Herb nor Jack would have confessed as much had they been accused.

The name of the millionaire's boat was Mermaid, and she was about as fine a specimen of the American boatbuilder's art as any of these amateur sailors had ever looked upon.

"Me for a swim before we have supper," said Nick; who felt rather dusty after tumbling around so many times during his exciting experience with the bull.

"I'm with you there, Buster," laughed Jack. "You know I've got an interest in your work, since I taught you how to swim while we were making that Mississippi cruise."

On the previous Fall, the high school in their home town was closed until New Year's by order of the Board of Health, on account of a dreadful contagious disease breaking forth. These six lads, having the three staunch motor boats, had secured permission from their parents or guardians to make a voyage down the Mississippi to New Orleans. Jack really had to be in the Crescent City on December 1st, to carry out the provisions of the will of an eccentric uncle, who had left him considerable property. The other chums had gone along for the fun of the thing. And it was this trip Jack referred to when speaking of Nick's swimming.

Presently both boys were sporting in the water, having donned their bathing suits. While thus engaged Jack noticed out of the corner of his eye that a boat had put out from the big vessel, and also that the two girls were passengers.

Perhaps they were going ashore to take dinner with friends at one of the cottages just beyond the end of the woods; although Jack fancied that the men rowing were heading a little out of a straight course, so as to come closer to the three little motor boats, and possibly give the fair passengers a better view of the fleet.

There was now a stiff wind blowing, something unusual at an hour so near sunset. The waves came into the bay from the south, it being somewhat open toward the lower end, and slapped up on the beach with a merry chorus, that made swimming a bit strenuous for the fat boy; though Jack, being a duck in the water, never minded it a particle.

Intent on chasing Buster, whom he had allowed to gain a good lead, Jack was suddenly thrilled to hear a scream in a girlish voice, coming from the boat which he knew was now close by.

His first thought was that one of the girls had leaned too far over the side, and fallen into the water, which at that point was very deep. And it was with his heart in his mouth, so to speak, that Jack dashed his hand across his eyes to clear his vision, and turned his attention toward the big power boat's tender.

CHAPTER III

THE BOAT IN THE FACE OF THE MOON

A single look told Jack another story, for after all it was no human life in peril that had given rise to that girlish shriek.

Upon the dancing waves he saw a pretty hat, which had evidently been snatched by the wind from the head of the golden-haired maid, who was half standing up in the boat, with her hands outstretched toward her floating headgear.

The men had started to change their stroke, and try and turn the boat; but with the wind blowing so hard this was no easy matter. The chances seemed to be that possibly the hat might sink before they could get to it.

Jack never hesitated an instant. No sooner did he ascertain how things lay than he was off like a shot, headed straight for the drifting hat. It chanced that the wind and waves carried it toward him at the same time; so that almost before the two men in the boat had turned the head of the craft properly, Jack was reaching out an eager hand, and capturing the prize.

"Hooray!" came in a chorus from the boys ashore near the fire. Even Buster tried to wave his hands, forgetting that he had full need of them in the effort to remain afloat, with the result that he temporarily vanished from view under a wave.

Jack smiled to see the two girls in the boat clapping their hands as they bore down upon him. He noticed now, that while the one who had lost her hat was slender and a very pretty little witch, her companion was almost as heavy in her way as Buster himself, and with the rosiest cheeks possible.

"Oh! thank you," cried the maiden whose headgear had been rescued from a watery grave. "It was nice of you to do that. And it was my pet hat, too. Whatever would I have done if it had sunk, with poor me so far away from our Chicago home. Is one of those dear little boats yours?"

"Yes, the one with the burgee floating at the bow," returned Jack, as he kept treading water, after delivering up the gay hat. "We're taking our vacation by making a trip from the Thousand Islands all through the Great Lakes. My name is Jack Stormways."

"And mine is Rita Andrews. My father owns that big power boat there; and we live in Oak Park near Chicago. This is my cousin, Sallie Bliss. I'm sorry to say that we're going to leave here early in the morning; or I'd ask you to come aboard and meet my father."

Nick meanwhile was approaching, making desperate efforts to hurry along before the boat passed on. For Nick had discovered that the rosy-cheeked girl was just the match for him, and he wanted to be introduced the worst kind.

Unfortunately the cruel men took to rowing again, and though Nick swam after, puffing and blowing like a porpoise, he was left in the lurch. But he succeeded in waving his hand to the departing ones, and laughed joyously when he saw that Miss Sallie actually returned his salute.

So the boat with its fair occupants passed away. Jack wondered whither the millionaire, whose name he remembered having heard before, was bound; and if a kind fate would ever allow him to see that charming face of Rita Andrews again. Little did he dream of the startling conditions that would surround their next meeting.

"Hi! there, you fellows, come ashore and get some duds on!" called George, who had been an interested observer of this little play.

"Yes," supplemented Josh, waving a big spoon as though that might be the emblem of his authority as "chief cook and bottle-washer," "supper's about ready, and my omelette eats best when taken right off the pan. Get a move on you, fellows."

It was amusing to see the scramble Nick made for the shore. The jangle of a spoon on a kettle always stirred his fighting spirit; he felt the "call of the wild" as George said, and could hardly wait until the rest sat down.

So the two swimmers went ashore, and hastily dressed. Nick was forever talking about the lovely roses in the cheeks of Miss Sallie.

"You didn't play fair, Jack," he complained. "When you saw how anxious I was to get up, why didn't you pretend to have a cramp, or something, to detain the boat. I didn't even get introduced. She don't know what my name is. It's mean, that's what I think."

Jack knew that Buster would never be happy unless he had some cause for grumbling. It was usually all put on, though, for naturally the fat boy was a good-natured, easy-going fellow, ready to accommodate any one of his chums to the utmost.

While they ate the fine supper which Josh spread before them, George entertained the party with a droll account of the adventure two of their number had had with a bull. He had purposely kept silent up to now, and bound Josh to secrecy, so that he could spring the story while they sat around.

Loud was the laughter as George went on in his clever way of telling things. But Nick laughed with the rest. Viewed from the standpoint of safety things really looked humorous now; whereas at one time they had seemed terrifying indeed.

"Catch me wearing that blessed red sweater again when I go for milk or eggs," he declared. "Once is enough for me. Oh! if I'd only had a camera along to snap Josh as he went climbing over that fence, with the bull so close behind. I'd get that picture out every time I felt blue, and laugh myself sick."

Josh assumed an injured air, as he spoke up, saying:

"Now would you listen to that, fellows? Just as if I looked a quarter as funny as Nick did, trying to scramble up that tree, nearly scared to death, because he thought Johnny Bull wanted to help him rise in the world. Oh! my land! but he was a sight. When I went off to get help I wanted to laugh so bad I just fell over in the grass, where he couldn't see me, and just had it out. Couldn't help it."

"That's what kept you so long, was it?" demanded Nick, reproachfully. "All right, the very next time you get in a pickle, and yell out for help, I'm going to get a crick in my leg when I try to run, see if I don't."

"All the same I noticed that you could swim to beat the band when you tried to join Jack, before the sweet girlies got away," put in George, maliciously.

"Nick was afraid the boat was going to upset, and he saw a chance to save that red-cheeked little dumpling from a watery grave," Herb remarked, with a grin.

"Suppose something had happened, Jack couldn't have rescued them both. But you can laugh all you want to, smarties, she waved her hand to me all the same, didn't she, Jack?" appealed the fat boy, stubbornly.

"I saw her wave to somebody, so I suppose it was meant for you," replied Jack.

"Birds of a feather flock together," chanted Josh.

"That'll do for you," Nick declared sternly. "She was a fine and dandy little lady, and I hope some time in the future I'll see Sallie Bliss again."

"Bliss! Oh! what d'ye think of that, fellows?" roared George.

"Leave Buster alone, can't you?" Jack said, in pretended indignation. "He's all right, and honest as the day is long. None of your Crafty Clarence in his makeup, you know, fellows."

Clarence Macklin was a boy who came from the same town as those around the camp fire. He was the son of a very rich man, who supplied him with almost unlimited spending money. Consequently Clarence was able to carry out any folly that chanced to crop up in his scheming mind.

Learning through trickery of the intention of the motor boat boys to cruise among the Thousand Islands, he had shipped his fast speed boat, called the Flash thither, and succeeded in giving them more or less annoyance. He was accompanied by his pet crony, a fellow called Bully Joe Brinker, who usually did the dirty work Clarence allowed himself to think up.

"Say, speaking of that fellow, wonder what's become of him?" George remarked; for there was a standing rivalry between his boat and that of the other, both being built solely for speed, and not comfort or safety.

"Didn't he hint something about coming up in this region later on?" said Jack.

"I understood it that way," observed Herb. "And more than a few times, while we cruised along the southern shore of Ontario and Erie, I thought we'd see his pirate boat bob up."

"I hope we don't run across that crowd again," observed Nick. "For they're sore on us, and bound to do us a bad turn if they find the chance."

"Well, we can keep our eyes open," remonstrated George. "You know Clarence believes that Flash can make circles around my bully boat, and I'm wanting to give him a chance to prove it."

"Chuck that, George," said Josh. "You know you beat him out once handsomely."

"Yes, but he said he hadn't tried to do his level best. Anyhow, if the chance comes again I'm ready to race him."

"How long would we be gettin' up till the Soo now, Jack, darlint?" asked Jimmie; who being second "high notch" in the line of eaters in the crowd, had been too busy up to now to do any great amount of talking.

"That depends pretty much on the weather," replied the leader of the expedition, who studied his charts faithfully, and was always ready to give what information he picked up, to his chums. "We are now something like one hundred and fifty miles sou'-east-by-south from Mackinac Island, where we expect to stop over a few days. If we pick out a good morning we ought to navigate the head of Huron and the crooked St. Mary's river to the Soo in one day. The steamers do, and we can make about as fast time."

"Of course we have to hold up for the Comfort pretty much all the way," said George; "not that I'm complaining, fellows, for I understand that it takes all sorts of people to make a world, and lots of different kinds of boats to please everybody. And in bad weather Herb and Josh fare better than the rest of us. Well, suppose we leave here tomorrow morning, if the weather lets us, Jack?"

"We will try and make Mackinac with just one more stop," Jack replied. "That will be easy enough; though if the wind gets around and the waves increase, we'll have to run for some snug harbor, George, because your boat and mine are hardly storm craft on these big lakes."

"It's been a foine trip so far, I say," observed Jimmie, reaching for another baked potato, which Josh had cooked to a turn in the ashes of the fire, somehow keeping them from blackening, as is usually the case in camp.

"You're right there, Jimmie," replied Herb. "And with no serious accidents to come, we'll make a record to be proud of. Just imagine us sitting around the fire in our cozy club house that is right now building, while Jack reads the stirring log of our experiences up here. It will make us live over the whole trip again."

"Yes," chimed in George, "and think of the bliss that must bring."

Nick colored a little, as he felt every eye on him.

"Look at the moon just peeping up over yonder, fellows," he observed, meaning to distract their attention.

"Just about full too," remarked Jack. "Going to be a great night for a camp."

"Makes me think of that moonlight race we had with the Flash," George went on, his heart always set on the matter of speed and victories.

Night was just closing in, and the grand full moon was rising from the watery depths, so it seemed.

"There comes a motor boat down yonder," remarked Herb. "See what a fine searchlight she has. No need of that, though, as soon as the moon gets fairly up."

"Say, she's just humping along to beat the band, I tell you!" declared Josh, as all eyes were turned to where the shadowy form of the advancing craft could be seen, growing plainer with every passing second.

"Oh! I don't know," instantly remarked George, who was unable to see much good in any small craft when his pet Wireless was around. "I should say she was doing just fairly, you know; but then she doesn't have to hold back for any elephant."

"That's a mean hit, George," said Herb, though he never changed his mind about his comfortable boat because of any slurs cast by his mates, who might come to envy him in bad weather.

"Look at her cut through the water, would you?" Josh went on. "The fellows aboard don't intend to turn in here to stop over. Must be in a hurry to get somewhere, I guess."

"There, she's just passing the rising moon. Why, I declare, fellows, seems to me she looks kind of familiar like!" Nick exclaimed.

Jack jumped up, and secured a pair of marine glasses. They were guaranteed for night work, and through them he could see the passing motor boat splendidly.

"Is it, Jack?" asked George, eagerly; and the other nodded.

"That's the same old Flash, all right," he said, looking around the circle.

"Gosh!" exploded Nick, "Crafty Clarence is on the trail once more, bent on revenge for the beat George gave his pirate motor boat. I see warm times looming up ahead of us, shipmates all. And ain't I glad I know how to swim now!"

CHAPTER IV

CAUGHT BY THE STORM

"I wonder if they know we are camping in this place right now?" Josh ventured.

"The chances are, they do," replied Jack. "Both of those chaps possess eyes as sharp as they make them. And there's another reason why I think that way."

"Then let's hear it, old fellow," begged Nick.

"This is a nice, attractive place to haul in, and spend the night, when cruising along in a small motor boat. As evening has come, not one in ten would think of passing the cove by; and you know it, boys," Jack went on, with emphasis.

"But they deliberately did that same thing," ventured Herb. "Yes, I get on to what you mean, Jack. They'd rather boom along, and take chances of being caught out on the open lake in the night, even with a storm in prospect, to stopping over near the camp of the motor boat club. Is that it?"

"Just what I meant, Herb," nodded the other.

"And I guess you struck it, all right," commented Josh.

"But if they didn't want to say us agin, what in the dickens did they iver kim up this way for, I doan' know?" remarked Jimmie, helplessly.

At that George laughed out loud.

"Wake up, Jimmie!" he exclaimed. "You're asleep, you know. Why, don't you understand that Clarence Macklin never yet took a beat like a fair and square man? He won't rest easy till he's tried it again with the Wireless. I happen to know that he hurried his poor old boat to a builder, and had him work on the engine, hoping to stir it up a peg or two. And now he's going to sneak around till he gets the chance to challenge me again."

"And," went on Nick, following up the idea, "he didn't want to drop in here with us, because in the first place he hates us like fun; and then he was afraid George might ask questions about his bally old boat."

"He wants to spring a surprise!" declared Josh. "That's his play all the time. When we had snowball battles, Clarence was forever hiding with a bunch of his men, and jumping out suddenly at us. That's where he got his name of Sneaky Clarence."

"Well," remarked Jack, "I hope George gets a chance to show him up again for the fraud that he is; but at the same time I don't want Clarence and

Bully Joe bothering us right along. We didn't come up here just to chase around after them."

"Or have the gossoons chasing around afther us, by the same token," laughed the Irish lad.

They sat around the fire, and carried on in their usual jolly way, telling stories, laughing, and singing many of the dear old school songs. Six voices, and some of them wonderfully good ones too, made a volume of sound that must have carried far across the bay to the cottages, where the summer residents were doubtless sitting out in the beautiful moonlight.

The boys began to think of retiring about ten or after. A couple of tents had been purchased after coming to the St. Lawrence river country; for somehow all of them became tired of sleeping aboard the boats, since there was little of comfort about it.

These tents had been erected under the supervision of Jack, who knew all about how a camp should be constructed, so that in case of wind or rain no damage was likely to result.

They made a pretty sight now, with the moonlight falling upon them, and the flickering fire adding to the picture.

Jack had wandered down to the edge of the water. The three motor boats were all anchored close by, and everything had been made snug; but of course it was not the intention of the boys to leave things unguarded. The chances of trouble were too positive to think of such foolishness.

"Too bad, Jack, that the wind has gone down," said a voice at his elbow; and turning Jack saw the grinning countenance of George.

"Oh! I don't know," remarked the other, slowly and cautiously, as if wondering whether George could read his secret thoughts, and know that he was just then thinking of the pretty little girl whose hat he had rescued from the hungry maw of the lake that afternoon.

"Why, I think I hear voices over yonder where they landed, and girls at that," George continued, wickedly. "No doubt the little darlings are about embarking on the return trip to the Mermaid. Now, if the wind would only suddenly swoop along, perhaps a boat might be upset. But Jack, with your clothes on, you'd have a tough time swimming out there and saving Rita's life, like you did her bonnet."

"Oh! let up on that, will you?" laughed Jack, good naturedly; for he was used to such joking and joshing on the part of his mates, and ready to take it in the same spirit of fun that it was meant. "I was thinking about our boats here. Seems to me that whoever is on guard should take up a position where he can keep an eye on the whole outfit. At the first sign of danger he must wake up the bunch of us. Isn't that right, George?"

"Sure it is; but see here, you don't really think anything will happen, do you?" the other demanded, uneasily. "Because if I had any idea that way, I'd feel like going aboard, and sleeping there, uncomfortable as a narrow speed boat is. Why, it'd nearly break my heart if anything knocked my Wireless just now, and spoiled the rest of my vacation."

"Oh! I guess there's no real danger," said Jack, quickly; "but you know my way of being cautious. An ounce of prevention, they say, George, is better than a pound of cure. We insure our boats against explosion and loss; why not do the same about our chances for a jolly good time?"

"Right you are, Jack. That's a long head you carry on your shoulders," admitted the skipper of the speed craft. "But there they come. I can see the boat, and the white dresses of the girls. She is a little angel, Jack, and seriously I don't blame you for wanting to see more of Miss Rita Andrews; but the chances are against you, old fellow."

"Well, girls were the last thing we had in mind when we started on this trip," remarked Jack. "We left lots of pretty ones at home, you know; and we're getting letters from some of them right along. There, they've made the big power boat all right, and are getting aboard."

"And you can go to sleep with an easy mind," laughed George, "because the young lady wasn't wrecked in port. But perhaps we might happen to catch up with 'em at the Soo, Jack. No doubt you had thought of that?"

"We expect to be at Mackinac first, and people generally stop off there a day or two," remarked the pilot of the Tramp, falling into the little trap shrewd lawyer George had set for him; whereat the other gave him a dig in the ribs, and ran off to the camp to get his blankets ready for his first nap.

But nothing out of the way did happen that night, though the motor boat boys kept faithful watch and ward, one of them being on duty an hour or more at a time up to dawn.

With the coming of the sun over the water all were awake, and preparations for breakfast underway. Jack, Nick and Josh concluded to take a morning dip, while the rest were looking after the cooking of a heap of delicious flapjacks done to a brown turn as only the wonderful Josh could coax them.

Smoke rising slowly from the big power boat's cook's galley pipe announced that preparations were underway there for an early start.

Indeed, the vessel started to leave the harbor even while Jack and his mates were still sitting around the fire, disposing of the appetizing mess that had been so skillfully prepared for the crowd.

"Jack, it's all right!" laughed George.

"Yes," chimed in Nick, innocently, with a sigh of relief, "they're heading north, sure as anything."

"Oh! we forgot there was a pair of 'em, sighing like furnaces," jeered Josh.

But Jack and the fat boy only laughed.

"Rank jealousy, Nick; don't you bother your head about such cruel remarks," said the former, winking to the stout youth.

"Well, everybody get busy now," said George, jumping to his feet. "It looks like we might have a fairly decent day, if that blessed old wind keeps away. My boat rolls like fun when in a wash, and I don't like it a bit. Hope we'll have the air out of the southwest today, so we'll be shielded by the shore."

He hurried off to get aboard. The others were not far behind, for tents had been taken down, and blankets stowed, while breakfast was being cooked; so that there was not a great deal to do now.

Then, after a last survey of the late camp had been taken by cautious Jack, in order to make sure that nothing was forgotten and the fire dead, he too stepped into his little dinky, paddled out to where Jimmie awaited him aboard the Tramp; and five minutes later the little flotilla started, amid a tremendous popping of motors, and much calling back and forth on the part of skippers and crews.

Once outside the protecting cape they headed due nor'-east by north, and kept just a certain distance away from the shore.

It was a lovely morning, and gave promise of a fine day; but these cruisers had learned through bitter experience never to wholly trust such signs. In summer at any rate, storms can develop with suddenness on the big lakes, and a squall start to blowing without warning. Hence they had adopted as a motto, the slogan of the Boy Scouts: "Be Prepared!"

George called out to the skipper of the Tramp, and pointed ahead, where, several miles to the north could be seen the dim shape of the big power boat, rapidly covering the distance that intervened between the cove and charming Mackinac Island.

"They'll be at Mackinac tonight, all right, Jack!" shouted George, who led the little procession in his speed boat.

Jack made no attempt at a reply; but Jimmie took up the cudgels at once.

"Sure we'll make it by tomorry night, if all goes well," he said; "and begorra, not wan of our boats is in the same class wid the big wan. Take the three togither and they'd be only a bite for the Mermaid. So we bate thim aisy now."

So they chugged along as time passed. In an hour all signs of the larger craft had passed from their sight. At noon they opened up Thunder Bay; and thinking to make the dangerous crossing of its broad mouth before having lunch, they kept on.

It was rather rough traveling, especially for the narrow Wireless; and acting upon Jack's suggestion George hovered close to the others, so as to have help in case of trouble, and be partly sheltered from the rollers by keeping in their lee.

But the passage was made in safety; and after that their course changed to some extent. The shore turned more toward the northwest, so that they headed into the wind, which was creating some sea, in which the small craft wallowed considerably.

An hour later Jack began to cast anxious glances toward the shore, hoping to discover an opening of some sort, in which the fleet might take refuge. For the sky was darkening by degrees, and he fancied he caught the muttering of thunder in the distance.

On their starboard quarter nothing could be seen but a vast heaving expanse of water; for Lake Huron at this point stretches more than fifty miles, before Grand Manitoulin Island is reached to the northeast.

It would be a bad place for such small craft to be caught in a storm. Still, the shore looked strangely devoid of any indentation, and Jack's fears increased as the minutes passed without any change for the better cropping up. But he did not express these aloud, and even his boatmate Jimmie, although often casting a look of anxious inquiry at the face of his skipper, could not tell what was passing in his mind.

And then, without any warning, there suddenly came a vivid flash of lightning over in the west, almost immediately followed by an ominous clap of thunder that seemed to make the very air quiver.

"Say, that looks bad!" called out Josh; who was in the cranky speed boat, and had more reason to be alarmed than most of his comrades.

"What shall we do, Jack?" asked Herb, whose Comfort was keeping close on the port side of the boat Jack had charge of.

"Push on for all we're worth," answered the other. "I think I see a harbor, if only we can make it before the storm breaks. George, you leave us, and drive ahead; for the danger is greater with you than the rest. But don't worry fellows; it's all right, we've just got to make that bay where the point sticks out, and we're going to do it too."

CHAPTER V

A STRANGE SOUND

George recognized the wisdom of such a move as his chum suggested. If the wind kept on increasing as it seemed bound to do, and the storm broke upon them in all its mid-summer violence, the cranky speed boat would be apt to feel the effect more than either of the other craft.

It was therefore of great importance that he and Josh seek the promised shelter with all haste. Much as he disliked leaving the balance of the fleet, necessity seemed to compel such a move.

Accordingly, he threw on all the motive power his engine was capable of developing, and began to leave the others quickly in the lurch.

Jack could easily have gone ahead of the heavy Comfort, but he did not mean to do so. Better that they stick together, so as to be able to render assistance if it were badly needed.

Talking across the narrow abyss of water separating the two boats was altogether out of the question, unless one shouted. There was no time for an exchange of opinions, since all of them needed to keep their wits on the alert, in order to meet the dangers that impended.

Already had the waves grown in size. They were getting heavier with every passing minute; and the little motor boats began to actually wallow, unless headed directly into the washing seas.

It was a critical time for all concerned, and Nick could be seen with his cork life-preserver carefully fastened about his stout body under the arms, as if prepared for the very worst that could happen.

It was about this time that Jimmie gave a shrill whoop.

"They done it!" he yelled, regardless of the rules of grammar, such was his delight. "The ould Wireless is safe beyant the p'int!"

Jack saw that what he said seemed to be so. The speed boat had evidently managed to reach a spot where the jutting tongue of land helped to shield her from the oncoming waves. She no longer plunged up and down like a cork on the water, though continuing her onward progress.

The sight spurred the others on to renewed zeal. If George could do it, then the same measure of success should come their way.

Five minutes later Jack noticed that there was an apparent abatement of the wild fury with which the heaving billows were beating against the bow of his little craft. A look ahead told him the comforting news that already was the extreme point standing between the two boats and the sweep of the seas.

"We do be safe!" shouted Jimmie; who, in his excitable way seemed ready to try and dance a jig then and there, an operation that would have been attended with considerable danger to the safety of the Tramp's human cargo.

"And not a minute too soon!" said Jack, as a sudden gust of wind tore past, that might have been fatal to his boat had it been wallowing in one of those seas just then.

As it was, they had about all they could do to push on against the fierce gale, protected as they were by the cape of land. The spray was flying furiously over that point, as the waves dashed against its further side. But the boys knew they were safe from harm, and could stand a wetting with some degree of patience.

George was waiting for them, his anchor down, at a point he considered the best they could make for the present. He had managed to pull on his oilskins, and was looking just like a seasoned old tar as the other boats drew in.

Jimmie and Nick were ready with the mudhooks, under the directions of their respective skippers. Hardly had these found a temporary resting-place at the bottom, than all four lads seized upon their rainproof suits, and presently they were as well provided against the downpour as George.

And the rain certainly did descend in a deluge for a short time. They had all they could do to prevent the boats from being half swamped, such was the tremendous violence with which the torrent was hurled against them by the howling wind.

But after all, it was only a summer squall. In less than half an hour the sun peeped out, as if smiling over the deluge of tears. The wind had gone down before, but of course the waves were still rolling very heavily outside.

"That settles our going on today!" declared George, as he pointed at the outer terminus of the cape, past which they could see the rollers chasing one another, as if in a great game of tag.

"It's pretty late in the afternoon anyhow," declared Josh, who was secretly worried for fear lest his rather reckless skipper might want to put forth again.

"Yes, and we might look a long way ahead without finding a chance to drop into a harbor as good as this," remarked Herb.

"You're all right," laughed Jack; "and we'd be sillies to even dream of leaving this bully nook now. Besides, if tomorrow is decent, we can make an extra early start in the morning, and get to Mackinac before dark."

"That suits me all right," Nick observed, as he complacently started to remove his oilskins, so that he could pay attention to the bulky cork life preserver, which he did not mean to wear all night.

They found that it was possible to make a point much closer to the shore, and it was decided to do so, especially after sharp-eyed Jimmie had discovered signs of a farm near by, possibly belonging to a grower of apples, since a vast orchard seemed to cover many acres.

"I hope that big power boat wasn't caught in that stiff blow," Jack remarked, as they were getting ready to go ashore in order to stretch their legs a bit and look around.

"Oh! I guess they must have made Mackinac," said George. "She was a hurry-boat, all right, and the wind would not bother her like it did our small fry."

"Thank you, George, for that comforting remark. I was really getting worried myself about the Mermaid," observed Nick.

"Listen to Buster, would you, fellows?" cried Josh. "I never thought he'd go back on the girls we left behind us, and particularly Rosie!"

But Nick only grinned as they joined in the laugh.

"I'm a privileged character now," he asserted, stoutly. "A sailor is said to have a best girl in every port, you know, fellows. And every one of you will agree with me that Sallie Bliss is as pretty as a peach."

"And just your size too, Buster," declared Herb.

"Look out for an engagement with some dime museum company as the fat"—started Josh; when he had to dodge something thrown at him by the object of this persecution, and the sentence was never completed.

The ground being sandy close to the water, they concluded to start a fire, so as to cook supper ashore, since it was so much more "homey" as Nick said, for them to be together at mealtimes. But all were of the opinion that it would be advisable to sleep on board.

"Another hot squall might spring up during the night," observed George, "and just fancy our tents going sailing off to sea. Of course I don't hanker about putting in a night in such cramped quarters as my narrow boat affords; but it can't come anywhere near what I went through with when Buster was my shipmate, down on the Mississippi."

"And then somebody ought to go after milk and eggs," suggested Herb.

"Here, don't everybody look at me," Nick bridled up. "I guess it's the turn of another bunch this time. Josh and myself have served our country as haulers of the necessities."

"But every farmer doesn't own a bull, Buster," remarked George.

"Well, I object to bulldogs just as much. Little fellows are all right, likewise pussy cats; but deliver me from the kind that hold on to all they grab. Nixey. You and Jack try it this time, George."

"That's only fair," spoke up the latter, immediately.

"Well," said George, "if we're going, the sooner we start the better; because you see the old sun is hanging right over the horizon."

"And I'm nearly caved in for want of proper nourishment," grumbled Nick.

No one paid any particular attention to his remark; because that condition was a regular part of his lamentations several times a day. The only time Nick seemed to be in a state of absolute contentment was the half hour following a gorging bee; and then he beamed satisfaction.

Accordingly the pair started forth, armed with a tin bucket for the milk. George had no great love for biting dogs himself, and as they approached the vicinity of the farm buildings he suggested to his companion that they arm themselves with stout canes, with which they might defend themselves in case of an emergency.

"Looks like a prosperous place, all right," Jack observed as they saw the buildings and the neat appearance of things in general.

"But seems to me it's awful lonely here," remarked George. "Where can the people all be? Don't see any children about, or women folks. Plenty of cows and chickens, but sure they can't take care of themselves."

"Well, hardly," laughed Jack. "We'll run across somebody soon. Let's head for the barn first. Generally at this time you'll find the men busy there, taking care of the horses, and the pigs."

"I hear hogs grunting," remarked George.

"Well, I got the same sound myself; but do you know it struck me more like a groan!" Jack said, in a voice somewhat awed.

"A groan! Gee; what do you mean, Jack?" exclaimed the other, turning toward his chum with a white face.

"Just what I said," Jack replied. "And listen, there it is again. Now I know it was no swine you heard, George. That sound was from the barn. Come on. I'm afraid somebody's in trouble here!"

CHAPTER VI

"CARRY THE NEWS TO ANDY!"

"Nobody here, Jack!" announced George, in a relieved tone, as the two entered the stable, and looked around.

A number of horses stood in stalls, munching their oats, which in itself told the observing Jack that some one must have been there a short time before, since the animals had been recently fed.

Before he could make any reply to his companion's remark, once more that thrilling sound came to their ears. And this time even George realized that it was unmistakably a human groan.

"It came from over here!" exclaimed Jack, as without the slightest hesitation he sprang across the floor of the place.

George following close upon his heels, saw him bending over the figure of a man, who was lying upon the floor in a doubled-up position.

"What has happened? Did one of the horses kick him?" gasped George, always a bundle of nerves.

"No, I don't think so," replied Jack. "I can find no sign of an injury about him. It's more likely a fit of some kind he's just recovering from. Lots of people are subject to such things, you know."

"Say, that's just what;" declared George. "I had an uncle who used to drop like a rock right in the street or anywhere."

"What did they do with him at such times?" demanded Jack, anxiously.

"Well, nobody seemed able to do much," replied the other. "I saw my father loosen the collar of his shirt, and lay him out on his back. A little water on his face might help; but in most fits it takes some time to recover. But I thought I saw his eyelids twitch right then, Jack."

"Yes, he's going to come out of it," replied Jack, as he managed to get the old man into what seemed like a more comfortable position.

And presently, as the two boys still bent anxiously over him, the man opened his eyes. He stared at them for a bit, as if trying to collect his thoughts. Then a horse neighed, and he seemed to realize his position.

Jack, seeing him trying to sit up, assisted him. The old man sighed heavily, and spoke in a weak tone.

"Reckon I dropped in my own stable that time. Might have been under the feet of the hosses too. And both men away. Who are ye, boys? I'm beholdin' to you more'n I can say," he went on.

Whereupon Jack soon explained how they belonged to a little company of cruisers who had been driven by the storm to take shelter behind the point of land; and that their present errand was to secure a supply of fresh milk and eggs, if so be they could be had.

"Help me to the house, please, boys," said the farmer, trying to rise. "I'm always some weak after one of these spells. They're acomin' oftener now, and I'll have to quit bein' alone. Now more'n ever I need Andy. Oh! if they can only find him for me, I'll be so happy."

Of course this was so much Greek to the two boys. But they gladly helped him to regain his feet, and walk to the house.

"The men will be back soon, and you can have all the milk and eggs you want!" he declared; and even as he spoke George discovered a team coming toward the farmhouse, evidently from some nearby town, with a couple of husky men on the wagon, which was piled high with new and empty apple barrels.

"That let's me out," laughed George, "for you see, I was just going to volunteer to milk Bossie; and as I've had mighty little experience in that line, perhaps she'd have kicked me into the next county for a bungler."

The men came on to the house, seeing strangers present, and Jack soon explained the situation to them. He learned that the old farmer's name was Jonathan Fosdick, and that the Andy he had spoken about was his only son, with whom he had quarreled several years back, and for whom his heart was forever yearning, now that old age and disease began to grip hold of him.

Supplied with the milk and the eggs the two lads started back to the camp.

"Promise to come up and see me again tonight, boys," the old farmer had pleaded, as he came to the door with them, after positively refusing to accept any pay for what they had received. "I want to speak with you about something that's on my mind a heap lately. You helped me once; p'raps ye can again."

"Now, what under the sun do you think he meant?" remarked George, as they plodded along with their heavy burdens toward the lake shore, where the boats lay.

"Just wait, and we'll know all about it soon," replied Jack; for while he could himself give a pretty good guess what was on the mind of Mr. Fosdick, he did not care to commit himself.

The others greeted the foragers with loud cries of delight.

"Then there wasn't any bull handy?" said Nick, with an evident shade of disappointment in his voice; for Nick was nothing if not generous; and having tasted the delights of being chased up a tree by an angry bovine, he felt that the other fellows ought to share the experience with him.

The fire was already burning briskly, and Josh employed in his customary tasks of getting things ready for cooking. At such times Josh was looked upon as a czar, and his simplest word was law. It was very pleasant for the tall, lanky lad to feel that he did have an hour or so each day, when every one bent the knee to his superior knowledge; and he certainly made the most of it.

And the supper was of course a bountiful one. It could not be otherwise so long as Nick and Jimmie had a hand in its preparation. The former hovered around from time to time, suggesting that Josh add just another handful to the rice that was being cooked, or possibly wondering if they could make one big can of mullagatawny soup do for six fellows; until frequently the boss would turn and wither him with a look, backed up as it was with that big spoon.

Later on, after everybody had declared themselves satisfied, Jack beckoned to the skipper of the Wireless.

"We promised that we'd run up and see how Mr. Fosdick was getting on, fellows," remarked the latter. "Be back inside of an hour or so; long before you are thinking of going aboard."

Nick started to rise, but sank back again as Jack shook his head.

"This farmer keeps a black bull, Buster. I saw him in an enclosure, and seemed to me the bars looked mighty slender!" observed George, maliciously.

"Excuse me, I think this fire feels mighty comfy," grinned Nick.

The two boys found Mr. Fosdick waiting for them. The woman who did his household work, a black mammy, had been over at a neighbor's when they were there before; but had later on returned, and cooked supper.

Things even looked a little cheerful, with the lamp-light flooding the comfortable livingroom of the big farmhouse.

"Sit down, boys," said the farmer, pointing to two chairs, he himself reclining on a lounge. "You're wondering now why I wanted to see ye again. I'm beholdin' to you for the prompt assistance you gave me. But there's somethin' more'n that. Did ye say as how ye was bound for Lake Superior way soon?"

"Why, we are going as far as the Soo," Jack replied, readily; "and we may take a notion to prowl along the northern shore for a short distance. I've always heard a heap about the big speckled trout to be taken around the mouth of the Agawa river and other places there, and since we have the chance I thought I'd like to try to land a whopper, if so be the rest of the boys are willing to go."

"The Agawa!" repeated Mr. Fosdick, eagerly. "I wonder if that might be the place now. 'Twas somewhere along that northern shore he said he saw my Andy."

"That was your son, I take it?" ventured Jack.

"Yes, my only boy or child. His mother died after he ran away, and I'm gettin' old now. I want Andy to come home; but try as I would, I never could get a line to him."

Then he went on to tell about his boy, and for a long time Jack and George had to listen to an account of Andy's childhood life. Gradually he came to the point where the highstrung boy had refused to be treated as a child any longer. A violent quarrel had followed, and Andy left home.

"I know now I was most to blame," said the old man, contritely; "and if only I could get word to my boy I'd beg him to come back to me. I want to see him again before I foller his mother across the great divide. Just a week ago I had a letter from a party who told me he was sure he saw Andy in a fish camp up on Superior. He'd growed up, and the gentleman didn't have a chanct to speak with him; but afterward it struck him who the man was. If so be ye run across Andy, tell him I'm waitin' with my arms stretched out for him, won't ye, boys?"

"To be sure we will!" declared George, heartily, for he was considerably affected by the appearance of grief on the old man's face.

They soon afterward started to say goodnight, wishing to get back to where the rest of the party sat around the camp fire.

"I forgot to tell ye," went on Mr. Fosdick, as he followed them to the door, "as they was a young chap here t'other day as said he'd keep an eye out for Andy. And now that I think of it, he had a little motor boat too, like them you tell me about. And he said he 'spected to cruise around Superior a bit."

George and Jack exchanged glances.

"And was his name Clarence Macklin?" asked the latter, quickly.

"Just what it was," replied the farmer, waving them a farewell.

"Now, what do you think of that?" asked George, as they strode on. "Why, that fellow is bound to crop up all the time like a jack-in-the-box. We can't even start to do a poor heartbroken old father a good turn, but he gets his finger in the pie. But there's a bully chance for me to get another race with his piratical Flash, and that's some satisfaction;" and Jack found himself compelled to laugh, realizing that George had his weakness just as well as Buster.

CHAPTER VII

TIED UP AT MACKINAC ISLAND

"All aboard!"

It was Nick who shouted this aloud on the following morning. They had arisen at dawn, and prepared a hasty breakfast. Josh had looked out for this on the preceding evening, for he had cooked a pot of grits, which being sliced while cold was fried in butter after being dipped in egg. Only several fryingpans were needed for the job, on account of the extreme fondness Nick had for that particular dish. But long ago his comrades had learned to view such an assertion on the part of the fat boy with suspicion; because it was discovered that the present treat was always the one Buster adored most.

The waves still seemed larger than might prove comfortable, but there was a fair chance of their going down later on in the day. Besides, George was gaining more confidence in his narrow boat, as he came to know it better; and he possessed something of a reckless spirit in addition.

"Ain't this just glorious!" exclaimed Nick, when they had gotten fully started, and passing beyond the protecting point, felt the full force of the waves.

Not a voice was raised in dissent; even Josh, while looking a little anxious, refused to put up a complaint as the Wireless ducked and bowed and slid along through the troubled waters like a "drunken duck," as Nick termed it aside to Herb.

But just as they had anticipated, things improved as the day advanced. The breeze grew lighter; and while it came over many miles of water, the sea was not threatening. Besides, there is such a thing as growing accustomed to such things. What in the beginning might excite apprehension, after a while would be accepted as the natural thing, and even looked upon with indifference.

They kept this up until after the noon hour, and splendid progress was made, so Jack declared. As he had been elected the commodore of the fleet, and kept tab of the charts, they always depended on what he said as being positive.

Finding a good opportunity to get ashore about this time the boys accepted it by a unanimous vote. So many hours aboard small boats gives one a cramp, and under such conditions a chance to stretch is always acceptable.

Their stay was not long, for all of them were anxious to reach the beautiful island known as Mackinac by evening. So once more the fleet put out, and in a clump bucked into the northwest breeze and the sea.

They were now heading due northwest, and about three in the afternoon George declared he could see land dead ahead which he believed must be Bois Blanc Island.

"I reckon now you're just about right," said Jack, after he had consulted his map, and then in turn peeped through his marine glasses. "For the way we head, there couldn't be any other land straight on. If that's so, fellows, we'll raise the hilly island just beyond pretty soon."

Before four they could get a sight of what seemed a little green gem set in the glittering sea of water.

"That's Mackinac, all right," observed George. "I can see white dots among the green, that stand for the houses. We're going to get there today, fellows. Told you so, Buster. Me for a juicy steak tonight then."

"Oh! don't mention it, please," gasped Nick. "You make my mouth fairly water. And if our boss cook would only suggest fried onions along with it, my cup of joy would be running over."

"Sure," called out Josh, "if you promise to peel the tear-getters. We need such a heap to satisfy that enormous appetite of yours, not to mention some others I know, that I refuse to undertake the job."

"Oh! all right; count on me!" cried Nick, looking around as though anxious to begin work at once, a proceeding that George vetoed on the spot.

"I need my eyes to see how to steer, thank you, Buster," he declared. "You just hold in your horses. Plenty of time. Besides, most of the onions are aboard the Comfort along with Josh."

An hour later they were approaching the magic isle that has won a fame all its own as a picture of beauty seldom equalled, and never excelled—green with its grass and foliage, and with many snow white cottages and hotels showing through this dark background.

"Did you ever see anything like it?" asked Jack, as the three boats sped onward.

"Never," replied several of the others.

"I'm glad we'll soon be there!" declared Nick; but everybody knew without asking, that he was thinking about that beefsteak and onions, rather than the joy of reaching such a pretty shore.

"Look at the old blockhouse up on the hill!" remarked Herb.

"Yes, I've been reading up on this place, and history tells about some lively times around here during the War of 1812. Seems the British thought

Mackinac a good place to have possession of. They sent out an expedition, and came ashore in the night, surprising the little American garrison."

"That was tough," grunted Josh. "Like to hear things the other way. Thought Americans never got taken by surprise."

"Oh! well," laughed Jack; "you want to read history again, my boy. But I notice a good many steamers around. I reckon most of those bound through to Chicago stop here, as well as the Lake Superior ones. There's a boat coming in full of people. The Islander she's called. That must be the boat going over to the Snow Islands every day. There's another back of her, perhaps coming down from the Soo. Seems quite a lively place, fellows."

"You bet it is. We must take a run around the island tomorrow, before going on. Never do to pass this by, as we may not be here again in a hurry," Herb remarked.

Approaching the shore they began to look out a suitable place where the small boats might be tied up for the time they expected to remain. This was not easy to find, since they had to take care and not get in the way of any large craft that might be going out.

After all it was Nick who discovered the opening. Josh declared that the fat boy's vision was sharpened by the clamorous demands of his appetite; but Nick, as usual, paid little attention to such slurs.

"Who's going ashore to find a butcher shop?" he demanded, as they began to draw close in to the shore, and get ready to tie up.

"I appoint you a committee of one to secure the steak," said Jack, solemnly; "and remember, don't let it be a bit over one inch thick, and weigh more than five pounds."

"Good gracious! that wouldn't be even a pound apiece!" expostulated Nick.

"All right! we expect to have some other things along with it, remember," Jack continued. "You know the penalty of disobedience to orders, Buster?"

"Deprived of food allowance for twenty-four hours!" broke in Josh.

Nick only groaned; and presently finding a chance to creep ashore he hurried off on his delightful errand. For when there was anything connected with meals to be done, Nick was as spry as anybody in camp.

It was some little time before he showed up again.

"Wow! look at what's coming, would you?" shouted Josh, suddenly.

Of course it was Nick, laden with various packages, and grinning amiably.

"It's all right, Jack," he announced as he came ambling along. "It doesn't weigh a fraction over five pounds. Oh! I was mighty particular about that, I tell you. Had him cut off pieces of the tail till it got down to an even thing."

"Here, somebody help him, or he'll take a header into the brink, and lose half of what he's hugging so tight!" called Herb, and Jimmie started to obey.

"But what's in all these other packages?" asked Jack, pretending to frown.

"Why, onions, just onions and then more onions!" came the bland reply; at which the others burst out into a roar, causing Nick to look at them in pity. "You fellows can laugh all you please," he said in lofty scorn; "it don't feaze me one little bit. I was afraid we might fall short, and so I bought a half peck at the butcher's. Then, while I was coming along, I saw some white ones, and couldn't resist the temptation to get a couple of quarts. They go fine raw when you feel just nippy, you see, along with a piece of pilot bread."

"But there's still another package; how about that, Buster?" asked George.

"Why," answered the other, slowly; "after I started off with the white ones would you believe it I discovered a lot of those fine big Spanish onions in a confectioner's store. I just couldn't resist the temptation to get half a dollar's worth. Mightn't have the chance again, you know, fellows. It's my treat this time."

"Thank goodness! we've really got enough of something to satisfy Pudding for once!" cried Josh, as he received the various packages.

"Look at the steak, Josh," said the provider, proudly. "Guess I ought to know a good thing in that line. It's streaked with fat, and is bound to just melt away in your mouth."

Josh admitted that it did look tempting; and later on the entire party agreed that Nick had profited by his hobby.

When starting upon this extended trip the motor boat boys had agreed that on no account would they sleep under the roof of a house, unless in case of sickness. So even at Mackinac they must keep to their boats.

Several of them went ashore to see what the place looked like under the electric lights, returning an hour or so later, ready for bed. Those left behind had attended to all necessary arrangements, so that little time was lost.

As customary, the watches were made up of two, on different boats, and so selected that Nick would be paired with Jack himself; because the commodore was suspicious of Buster's ability to remain awake with any one else as his sentry mate.

It happened that while these two were taking the first turn, and Jack every once in a while would poke Buster with a setting pole he kept handy, something not down on the bills came to pass. The first thing that Jack knew about it was when Nick gave vent to a shrill screech, and scrambled to his knees, holding on to some struggling object that seemed to scratch and snarl and act in a way that was altogether mysterious. And of course the whole six boys were immediately awake, sitting up to ask all sorts of questions.

CHAPTER VIII

GEORGE WAITS FOR HIS CHUMS

"What is it?" Josh exclaimed, as he scrambled to his knees.

"Buster is on the rampage again! That's what comes of eating too much supper. He's got a bad case of indigestion, I bet!" declared George, grumblingly; for he had come very near falling over the side of his boat when Josh made that sudden move, and it startled him not a little.

"But he's got hold of something, I tell you! Look at him grabbing around. Must be a wildcat or something like that," Josh went on.

"Faith ye're all wrong," spoke up Jimmie. "Sure it's a monkey he's huggin' till his breast, so he be."

"A monkey!" cried Herb, as he appeared behind the fat boy, holding a fryingpan threateningly in his hand.

"Yes, that's what!" gasped Nick. "Don't you see, a tame monkey, and with a little red cap, and a coat on. He was going through my pockets, I tell you, when I woke up—that is when I first felt him. Give us a hand here and help me hold the little scratcher. My! but he's strong, and he tries to bite my nose every time."

"Because you're hurting him," said Herb. "Wait till I get hold of that bit of rope he's trailing behind. Now let him loose, Buster, but keep him away from your face. He'd scratch your eyes out."

The queer little visitor seemed to be willing to submit, once Nick stopped squeezing him; for he immediately took off his red cap, and made quite a bow. Then he snatched up a small tin cup that was attached to a belt he wore, with a tiny chain, and held it out to Herb.

"Give him a penny, Herb," laughed Jack.

"Yes, he recognizes an old acquaintance; help a poor fellow in distress, Herb!" Josh hastened to add.

"Where under the sun d'ye suppose he came from?" asked George, suspiciously.

"Must belong to some Italian organgrinder, I should say, judging from the uniform, and the piece of broken rope. Perhaps he's run away, and wanted to become a stowaway on board Herb's boat," Jack went on.

"All right," the other remarked, promptly, "anyhow, he knew a good boat when he saw one. Give him credit for that. But did you hear what Buster said about him feeling in his pockets? Now, I've heard it said that often these monkeys are taught to steal, going up into second-story windows, and grabbing things. Perhaps he was sent aboard right now to pick up anything he could find."

"I tell you he knew all about vest pockets, as sure as you live," announced Nick.

"Looks to me as if he had got something in his pocketbook right now!" declared Herb.

"What's that? A monkey have a pocketbook? You're poking fun at us!" cried Josh.

"I am, eh? You observe me," said Herb, as with a dextrous movement he seized upon the monkey, and by main strength forced him to eject something from his mouth.

"Say, it's a real watch, fellows!" cried Nick, astonished; "he had it right in his cheek, sure he did."

"And it's my little dollar nickel watch," said Herb. "Shows he searched me before trying Buster. All the same if it'd been a hundred dollar gold repeater. He's a thief, sure enough. What'll we do with him, fellows?"

"Tie him up, and if nobody comes after him, we'll keep Jocko," suggested Josh.

"Think he'd be lots of fun, I suppose," grumbled Nick. "But if he stays it's got to be on another boat than this. The little fiend would have it in for me. He'd worry the life out of me; and I just can't afford to lose any flesh."

"Changed your tune, eh?" taunted Josh. "Seems to me I've heard you trying all sorts of ways to get thin."

"That was before I took notice of the horrible example we had along, of the living skeleton," retorted Nick. "After that I just made up my mind to remain nice and plump. Some people look best when they're fat, you know."

"There, he's thinking of Sallie again," remarked Josh.

"But we haven't seen a sign of the Mermaid," remarked George; "and I reckon she's left here for the Soo region ahead of us. But Herb, find some way to fasten the little rascal up for tonight, so he can't do any mischief. If his owner comes for him in the morning we'll give him a scare."

Herb managed to do this, although Nick declared he would be afraid to take a wink of sleep for fear of being choked, or something else as dreadful. All the same when his time came to give up sentry duty, no one heard so much as a "peep" from Nick again until daylight arrived.

It was arranged on the following morning that they should explore the island, in order to see its wonders and beauties, in two detachments, each consisting of three. Jack learned that bicycles could be hired close by, and mounted on these he and Herb and Josh made the grand rounds, allowing nothing to escape them.

Then after lunch the others took wheel and carried out the same programme, even to visiting the old blockhouse on the hill, and viewing the charming marine spectacle from the top of the little bluff.

As they gathered around late in the afternoon to compare notes, and discuss the various matters that interested them, Jack noted first of all that the shrewd little monkey, which had been dubbed Jocko, was still aboard the Comfort.

Nobody had shown up to inquire about him. Nick was for going ashore and spreading the news of the find far and wide; but the others refused to allow him. They really believed that Jocko had been sent aboard by his master to steal; and that this party was afraid to claim him now.

"If we have to take him along he'll give us lots of fun," remarked Jack.

"Yes, Buster is only thinking that there'd be one more mouth to feed, and that might cut his share of the rations down a peg," asserted Josh.

"Now that's where you wrong me," declared the fat boy, solemnly. "If you insist on hearing what I was thinking about, I'll tell you. Suppose we should get stormbound somewhere up on the twisting St. Mary's river, or on the biggest fresh water lake in the world—why, you see we could always turn to Jocko, and make a good meal. I remember reading that monkeys were just prime."

"Oh! you cannibal!" cried the horrified Josh. "Why, that poor little innocent looks just like a baby."

"Yes," retorted Nick, "your mother showed me your picture when you were six months old, and there is a close resemblance."

Night came on, and there was no claimant, so Jocko ate supper with the boys. He was already making good friends, and seemed very well satisfied with his new lot. Perhaps he missed the cuffing and beating he was accustomed to; but he could do without that very well; and the eating must have appealed to him strongly.

In the morning they left soon after breakfast. The day opened fair, and they knew there was a long trip before them if they hoped to cross the head of Lake Huron, and follow the winding channel of the St. Mary's river so as to reach Sault Ste. Marie by night.

Fortunately the breeze, what little there was, chanced to be in the north for a change. This allowed them to keep close to the southern shore of the peninsula for some hours, following its contour and avoiding the pounding that heavy seas always brought in their train.

Finally they entered the narrow strait between the mainland and big Drummond Island. Here the bustling port of Detour was passed. Nick hinted about going ashore and doing a little marketing; but Jack vetoed that proposition.

"Plenty of time to do all that after we get to the Soo tonight," he observed; and Nick knew there was no appeal from his decision.

"Is that Canada over yonder?" asked Josh, pointing to the island off their lee.

"No, Drummond belongs to Michigan," Jack replied. "Further on though, we'll strike St. Joseph's Island, and that is a part of Canada. So we'll all step ashore just to say we've been outside the U. S. for once."

"And that Mud Lake you were telling us about is somewhere along there, ain't it?" Herb asked.

"We'll find it, I reckon," replied the commodore, drily.

They did, and had reason to remember it too. Sometimes the waterway bearing the outlet of Lake Superior to the lower lakes was very wide and imposing. Then again it would narrow until Nick expressed his firm conviction that they had taken the wrong channel, and would be stopped, and have to return over their course.

But Jack kept his charts before him as he led, and was positive he had made no mistake of that sort. Occasionally George would be unable to restrain his impetuous nature. At such times he would shoot ahead of the others, to make a little rush of perhaps a mile, and then slow up to await their coming, being always careful not to lose sight of his chums.

But alas, George did this prank just once too often. He heard Jack say some time before that they were passing through Mud Lake, and must be careful; but thought this referred to getting lost in some side passage that looked promising.

"Wait up at the head yonder; you're too slow for me!" he called out, as the Wireless left the bunch, and cut through the water like an arrow shot from an archer's bow.

"Lookout!" warned Jack; but George who was quite confident concerning his own ability to manage his affairs, just waved a hand back, and continued to speed for all his racing boat was worth.

Jack was sitting there where he could manage the wheel and continue to study the chart spread in front of him, when he heard a wild whoop from Jimmie.

"Look! look yander!"

Jack was just in time to see poor Josh take a flying header into the water, when the speed boat came to an abrupt stop on a concealed mudbank.

The sound of the tremendous splash floated back to the ears of the others, causing Nick to roll over, and make the boat quiver with his riotous laughter; for that Josh should be the victim of this ridiculous accident gave the fat boy exceeding great joy.

CHAPTER IX

IN TERRIBLE PERIL

"Just what I expected!" exclaimed Jack, grimly.

"What was it?" demanded Herb; for at the moment it happened that the Tramp, being in front, obstructed the vision of those in the larger boat.

"Oh! tell me, was that really poor old clumsy Josh?" demanded Nick, poking his red face over the side of the Comfort. "I saw a pair of legs up in the air, and remembered some fellow down at Mackinac telling us what big frogs they found up here along the St. Mary's. The bass just love them, he said, and the bigger the frog the larger bass you get. That one would take in a whale, I guess, eh?"

"It was Josh all right, for I can see George trying to get him with his boat hook right now," said Jack, hardly knowing whether to laugh, or feel provoked on account of the possible delay.

"But why did Josh jump? Was he practicing stunts?" Nick went on innocently.

"Well," replied the commodore, "I imagine George made him squat up in the extreme bow, to sing out if he saw a shallow place ahead. And evidently Josh was looking all around, for he failed to discover a mudbank that was just hidden under the surface of the water."

"But George found it," asserted Herb.

"Trust George for findin' annything at all, at all," grinned Jimmie.

"Hope he didn't go to busting his old engine again. My! what a terrible time we did have with that cranky thing on the Mississippi," observed Nick; who had been on board the speed boat during that memorable cruise down to New Orleans, and hence passed through an experience he would never, never forget.

"I hope not," echoed Jack. "Perhaps the worst is yet to come. Perhaps he ran on that old mudbank so hard, going at top speed as he was, that he won't find it an easy job to work off again."

"That might delay us, be the powers, so we wouldn't be able to pull into the ould Soo short of tomorry, bad cess till hasty George!" remarked Jimmie.

"Well," remarked Nick, with a contented sigh, "at the worst we've got Jocko, you remember, boys. Baked or stewed he'd make a meal for the crowd."

Meanwhile they were rapidly drawing closer to the stuck Wireless. Apparently the skipper of the stranded craft had succeeded in dragging his crew out of the mire, for there was a dripping figure on the forward deck, scraping the mud away, and evidently more or less bubbling over with various remarks.

Jack cautioned Herb to slow down as they drew near.

"Bad enough to have one held fast," he said. "If the whole bunch got stuck, why, we'd have to take to the dinkies, and go ashore on Canada soil. How does your engine work, George? Nothing broken I hope?"

"I don't think so," came the reply from George who looked somewhat humiliated, as does every sailor when held up on a mudbank.

"Give it a try, and see. Reverse, and perhaps you'll glide off backwards, the same way you went on," Jack suggested.

At any rate the engine worked apparently as well as ever; but though George put it at its "best licks," as he declared, there was not a sign of anything going.

Josh tried to use the setting pole, and came very near taking another header.

"Say, this mud goes right along down to China, I reckon; leastways there ain't any bottom to it!" he cried, as he recovered himself just in time.

"We'll take your word for it, Josh," said Nick, sweetly; "because you know you've been over to see for yourself. But I wouldn't try it again. Next time perhaps you might stick your head in and smother. Then what would I do for any fun at all?"

George kept trying every way he could think of, in the effort to work his boat off the bank of sticky mud. It was in vain. Apparently many unseen hands held it tight, as though unwilling to let the reckless skipper have another chance.

When an hour had passed, with several false alarms, as George thought success was coming, he turned to Jack with a blank face, upon which disgust was plainly written.

"You'll have to get me out of this, commodore," he said. "I own up that I don't seem able to budge her a bit. Even with Josh in the dinky, pulling like all get-out, and her engine rattling away at full speed astern, she won't move an inch. And already we've lost enough time to make it impossible to get to the Soo by night."

George was apparently penitent, so Jack did not have the heart to rub it in at that time. Later on perhaps he might force the reckless one to promise about turning over a new leaf.

"All right; we'll soon yank you out of that, George. I didn't want to propose anything until you had tried every scheme you could think of. Herb, throw George your painter, and let him make fast to the stern of the Wireless. Then I'll do the same by you. In that way we'll be able to get both boats working. If George starts his engine at the same time, she's just got to come off, or go to pieces. Get what I mean?"

"Sure I do, and it's a good idea," replied the pilot of the Comfort, readily.

Of course George was willing enough to accept any sort of assistance now. And he readily made the painter fast to a ringbolt at the stern of the speed boat.

When all things were ready, Jack asked him to get his engine moving.

"Now, start yours up slowly, Herb," Jack went on; "not too fast to begin with; but gradually increase until you're applying two-thirds of your power. Stop there, and if she refuses to budge, I'll come in. We'll get her yet. She's got to come, I tell you."

And she did, after the Tramp added her drawing facilities to those of the others.

"Hurrah!" shrilled Josh, when the speed boat started to move backwards out of her muddy berth; he had almost plunged over again, and saved himself by a quick clutch at a cleat near by.

"What next?" asked Herb, after they had become disentangled again, and were in a condition to proceed.

"No use thinking of making the Soo today," remarked Jack. "Too dangerous along the upper reaches of this river to try it in the night. We can move along to the upper end of this island, and camp on Canadian land tonight, for a change."

"That sounds good to me," observed Nick; but only suspicious looks were cast in his direction; for well they knew that the word "camp" with Buster was another way of spelling "eat."

"How far would we be from the city at the rapids, then?" asked Herb, as they once more started.

"Oh, we could make it in a few hours," Jack replied, "if all went well. Keep to the right of that smaller island. That belongs to Michigan. Some use the other channel; but we'll take this one. You see, St. Joseph's Island is all of fifteen miles long, and pretty wild in parts. Ought to be good hunting here in season."

"Don't I wish it was in season, then," said Nick, smacking his lips. "Always have wanted to eat some venison from Canada right in camp. Say, fellows, if a silly old deer just went and committed suicide before our very eyes, by jumping over a precipice, wouldn't we have a right to get a haunch from his bally old carcase?"

"Well," laughed Jack, "if a Canadian game warden found you in possession he'd take you in. So just forget all you've ever heard about juicy venison. It's dry and tough stuff at the best, and couldn't compare with that Mackinac steak you bought."

Nick sighed.

"And we have to wait till tomorrow noon before we are in touch with a market, do we? I don't ever see how we're going to pull through. Tell you what, somebody ought to try for fish here when we stop. Looks like bass might hang around waiting for a chance to jump into the pan. How about that, Jack?"

"Just what I had made my mind to try," smiled the other, who liked nothing better than bringing his rod into play when there was a chance for game fish.

After a while George announced that he could see what looked like the end of the big island ahead.

"And here's a pretty decent place to pull in," declared Herb.

As they had nothing to fear from storms or hoboes in such a retired nook, the boys, having secured their boats in proper fashion against the shore, where they could not rub or get into trouble, amused themselves as they saw fit.

Jack, true to his promise, got out his fishing tackle, and proceeded to try all sorts of lures in the hope of tempting a bass to bite. Finally he took his little dinky, and began to troll, using a phantom minnow. Almost immediately he had a vicious strike, and after a struggle pulled up a fine fish.

"Do it some more!" called out Herb, who was lying on the shore, watching him at the sport.

Five minutes afterward Jack duplicated his feat, only this was even a larger fish than the first. So the time passed. Josh was busily engaged near the tents which he, Herb and George had erected; while Jimmie was doing something aboard the Tramp.

"Where's Nick?" asked Herb, after a long time had elapsed. "I hope the silly fellow hasn't gone and lost himself now. A fine time we'd have hunting that fat elephant through all that bush."

"He was here only a little while ago," remarked George, looking up.

"Looky yander, an' ye'll see him!" exclaimed Jimmie; "over beyant that dead three. Sure, he do be sneakin' up on something or other, and thryin' till coax it till kim till him. I say the baste now. Oh! murdher! by all the powers, somebody call out till him to sthop it!"

"Why, what's the matter with him?" asked Josh, coming to life at the prospect of perhaps seeing his rival for high honors in the farce line duplicate his ridiculous feat of taking a header into the mud and water.

"Look at him, would ye, the crazy wan!" gasped Jimmie, "thryin' till coax a baste loike that!"

"Is it Jocko?" queried Josh, unable to catch sight of the other just then.

"The little monk ye mane?" replied Jimmie. "Och! that would be aisy now. It's tin times worse than that. Call till him, Herb; I'm that wake I can hardly spake above a whisper. 'Tis a terrible danger he be in, for the animal is a white and black skunk; and poor innocent Nick, I do belave he thinks it be a pretty pussycat!"

CHAPTER X

MAROONED

"Leave it alone, you Buster!"

"Get behind a tree, quick!"

"Run, Buster, run for your life! It'll get you!"

George, Herb and Josh sent these warning cries at the top of their voices. As to whether the object of their combined concern heard, there could be no reasonable doubt; for Nick immediately waved one of his fat hands disdainfully toward them. Evidently he imagined that his chums were envious of his great good luck in finding so splendid a chance to annex a beautifully striped real Canadian pussy cat.

"Oh! murdher!" ejaculated Jimmie, "look at the rickless fellow, would ye? Sure, he manes to grab it, so he do!"

"But he won't, all the same!" cried George, grimly.

Since shouting and gesturing seemed to have no effect upon the imperiled youth, all the four boys could do was to stand there, holding their breath, and watching the dreadful developments. Nor was that the first time or the last that they found occasion to hold their breath.

Nick by now believed that he had wheedled enough, and was within proper striking distance. They saw him make a sudden forward swoop, with extended arms, as if bent upon giving the intended victim no possible chance of escape.

"Wow!" yelled George, as he saw Nick stop short, throw up his arms, and almost fall to the ground.

One terrified look Buster gave the object of his recent admiration. Then turning, he ran as well as he could toward camp, gripping his nose with both hands.

"Keep off!"

"Don't you dare come near us, do you hear!"

"Now you've gone and done it, Buster! That's what you get for wanting to bake poor little Jocko!"

George, as if in desperation, jumped over and picked up his gun.

"Stop where you are!" he cried. "We're willing to talk this thing over; but at a proper distance, do you hear, Buster?"

Poor Nick was aghast. Almost overpowered by the terrible fumes as he was, it looked like adding insult to injury when his own chums turned against him, and refused to let him enter the camp.

He did come to a halt some thirty feet away, and with one hand, clung to a sapling; while the other was trying to keep the powerful scent from smothering him.

"What can I do, fellows?" he asked, pitifully.

George was almost bursting with laughter, but pretended to look as stern as his father when serving in his capacity as judge of the court.

"First promise that you won't attempt to enter the camp without permission!" he demanded.

"I promise you, sure I do," groaned Nick swaying weakly alongside his support.

"Jimmie," went on George, "you go and call Jack in, if he isn't on the way here already, after all this racket. We want everybody to have a hand in deciding Buster's fate."

"Good gracious!" cried the wretched Nick, "what d'ye mean, George? Do I have to be shot, because I made a little mistake? I give you my word I really thought it was a Canada species of cat. And if we had to have a menagerie along with us, I was going to match her against your monkey. Oh! why didn't I think? I ought to have known better. It was awful, fellows; shocking I tell you!"

"I agree with you, Buster," remarked George, putting his fingers up to his nose, "please go a little farther away. We can talk better then."

Jimmie had hardly reached the shore before he started back. And Jack was seen following close behind. Evidently, then, the fisherman must have heard the loud outcries, and speeded his little boat for the landing, anxious to know what could have happened to Nick.

He had no need to be told. One hardly required to be within sixty feet of poor Buster to understand the entire story. Jack did not laugh though doubtless later on the incident would afford him more or less merriment. It was a serious matter, as he well knew, and must affect every one in the party.

"Jack," called out Nick, looking beseechingly at the commodore of the fleet, "take my part, won't you? They want to shoot me, or do something as bad, just because I didn't know the gun was loaded. Please take that thing away from George. He looks so fierce I'm afraid of him!"

So Jack, to ease the mind of the fat boy, who was really shivering with anticipation of dire results springing from his blunder, did take George's gun from his unresisting hands, and laid it aside.

"But Jack!" exclaimed Herb, "something's just got to be done. We can't bear to have him in camp with us, you know, after this. And think of me having to stand for that dreadful smell day after day. Wow! it would knock me out. I'd want to jump over in the deepest part of Lake Superior."

"I don't see what can be done," said George, "except to maroon him here on this foreign island until we come back again. By that time perhaps it won't be so very bad. Herb can keep him in the dinky towing behind, and stand it."

At that poor Nick set up a fresh howl.

"Don't you dare think of doing that," he cried, shaking his fat fist at the author of the suggestion. "Why, I'd starve to death in no time; not to speak of being devoured by the wild beasts. Think up some other way, won't you, please, Jack? Don't listen to George. He's got it in for me because I gave him so much bother on that Mississippi cruise. I want you to fix it up, Jack. You'll know how."

Jack still looked very grave.

"Well, you understand that in a case of this kind only desperate remedies will do, Buster?" he began.

"Yes, yes, I know;" whimpered the other, "and I'm willing to do anything you say, Jack; but don't leave me here over in a Canadian wilderness. It ain't human, that's what!"

"All right," Jack proceeded, solemnly, "if you give me your solemn promise to obey. First of all you must strip off every bit of clothes you have on."

Nick began at once, and with eagerness.

"Will it wash out, then? Oh! I can rub like a good fellow, I promise you; only give me a chance!" he exclaimed.

"All the washing in the world wouldn't take that scent out," George declared.

"There's only one way, and that is to bury the clothes!" said Jack.

"What?" gasped the astonished Nick; "and me go naked? Good gracious! Jack, I just can't do that! Make it easier for me, won't you? Why, I'd get my death of cold. Besides, what would I do when we got to the Soo? Please tell me something else."

At that the boys could hold in no longer, and a shout told that they were beginning to see the comical side. But Jack waved his hands.

"Be still!" he said, sternly. "This is no laughing matter. Never fear Buster, but you'll be able to rake up enough clothes to last till we get to the Soo, where you can buy a new outfit. Off with every stitch, now. Then you must dig a hole and bury them; or else carry the lot deep into the bush here, as you choose."

"Is that all?" asked Nick, tremulously, as he hastily tore the last remnant of his garments from his stout person.

"Not quite," replied Jack. "Get rid of the stuff next. Then come back to where you are now. I'll be waiting for you with a pair of short scissors I happen to have along with me; for you see I've just got to cut all your hair off!"

"Oh! what a guy I'll be, Jack," moaned poor Nick. "I'll sure never hear the last of this thing."

"Think of us!" said George, sternly, "how we must remember it for days and days. You're getting off dirt cheap, Buster, let me tell you. I've heard of fellows who had to live like hermits in the woods for weeks."

"Now get busy," observed Jack. "The boys will be rooting out your bag, and I'll fetch what clothes we can gather to you. We must do all we can to smother this perfumery factory."

"Yes, be off wid ye!" said Jimmie, bent on having a hand in the game.

Nick stared mournfully at the clothes on the ground. Then he slowly gathered them up in his arms. They noticed that as he walked away he looked around with exceeding care at every step he took, as though not for worlds would he want to renew his acquaintance with that pretty striped Canadian pussy cat.

Jack was as good as his word. When George and Herb had collected an outfit calculated to serve poor Nick until they reached a land of plenty, and clothing establishments, he carried the lot to the place appointed.

Here came Nick presently with a most dejected air; and groaning in spirit the fat boy allowed the other to shear off all his abundant locks.

He certainly did look like a guy when the job was completed, for Jack made no pretentions towards being a barber, and there were places that had the appearance of being "chopped with an axe," as George privately declared later, when viewing the work of the commodore.

After that they made Nick take a long bath. Indeed he thought he would never get out of the water, and his teeth were chattering before the embargo was finally raised.

Fortunately that wonderful red sweater which had attracted the bull toward the wearer not so very long since, had been safe aboard at the time of his recent mishap, so that Nick could depend on its warmth. He was grateful for small favors just then; and quite subdued for a whole day; though nothing could keep a buoyant nature like his in subjection long.

Of course he would never hear the last of the joke, and must stand for all manner of scoffing remarks, as well as uplifted noses when he came around. But Nick would live it down in time.

And no doubt, when the account of the cruise was read over during the next winter, Nick would join in the general laugh when he discovered that Jack had called this temporary stopping place on Canadian soil "Kitty Kamp."

It was night before Nick was allowed to come into camp; and even then they made him do penance by sitting off in a corner by himself, "just like I was a leper," as he declared, though bound to submit to the indignity.

But "it's an ill wind that blows nobody good," and at least Nick escaped guard duty that night, for nobody wanted to sit up with him.

George declared that the very first thing he meant to purchase when he arrived at the city at the rapids was a bottle of violet water, with which he could saturate himself for a season.

But by morning the terrible effect had in part died away; though possibly familiarity bringing about contempt may have had considerable to do with their noticing the disagreeable scent less.

Of course all of them were glad to get away from that camp. To Nick in particular its memory would always evoke a shiver. When brought to book in connection with the adventure he always declared that it was what a fellow got for wanting to invade foreign countries, and meddle with unfamiliar animals belonging there.

But Jack and the others felt sure that Buster from that day forth would know the great American skunk a mile off, and shy at a closer acquaintance.

They got away at a reasonable time, and continued their northern progress through the crooked St. Mary's River. On the way they saw numerous nooks that aroused the sportsman spirit in Jack; for he just knew the gamy bass lurked in those inviting waters, awaiting the coming of the fisherman. But there was no time to spend just then in seeking sport.

At about eleven o'clock they passed the smaller rapids, a most picturesque spot, where the water rushed boiling through many channels, and innumerable lurking places for the spotted trout seemed to invite a stay. But the Soo was now close at hand, and all of them were eager to look upon the famous big rapids, unexcelled for beauty and grandeur in all the land.

When the three motor boats presently reached a point where the little city on the left hand shore as well as the foamy rapids, and the railroad bridge stretching from Canada to the Michigan bank, came into view, the boys involuntarily waved their hats, and sent forth a cheer.

CHAPTER XI

DOWN THE SOO RAPIDS

"Alabama! here we rest!" cried George, as they kept booming along up the strong current of the river, until a spot was reached just below the foot of the rapids.

Not many steamers stop at the Soo, save those which run in connection with the tourist travel, between Mackinac and the rapids city. But there is a constant procession of steamers, and whaleback grain barges going in both directions, day and night, all during some seven months of the year. The tonnage of the government canal through which these boats pass around the rapids far exceeds that of the Suez Canal for the entire twelve months.

After finding a responsible party in whose charge the three brave little boats could be left, the cruisers proceeded to take in the sights.

Of course the rapids came first, and they viewed these from every angle. Jack was also deeply interested in the government fish hatchery on the little island; and watched with an envious eye the various pools in which scores of enormous speckled trout, weighing upward of seven pounds, were kept.

"Wait till we get to the Agawa," he said, shaking his head with determination. "I want to find out how some of those whoppers feel at the end of a line."

Nick had made for a clothing emporium, where he fitted himself out in some new clothes. Of course he did not explain just why this was necessary; but judging from the suspicious looks cast upon him every time he came near the clerk, the latter could give a shrewd guess concerning the truth.

Jack was still watching some of those giant trout jump out of the water in the pool when he dangled a long blade of blue grass so as to make the feathery end touch the surface like a fly, when George joined him; for they had settled upon the hatchery as a sort of rendezvous where they could come together, so as to take the thrilling ride down the rapids in a big Indian canoe.

"All off, Jack!" said George, trying to look sober; though there was a merry twinkle in his black eyes that belied the solemn cast of his face.

"What do you mean?" asked the other. "Anything more happened to that fellow Buster? Or perhaps it's Josh who's bent on halting our expedition now, with some caper. Go on, tell me."

"Oh! you're away off," grinned George. "I only meant to inform you that they're gone on ahead of us."

"I suppose you mean the Mermaid," Jack remarked.

"That's right," George responded, promptly. "Left here this very morning for a cruise through the Big Lake. Went through the canal about breakfast time. Seems as if we're just bound to keep tagging at their heels, don't it, Jack? I suppose we'll hear a howl from Buster now, because he is cheated out of seeing that fat Miss Sallie again."

"Buster has enough to think of in other directions, I suspect," smiled Jack.

"Well, I should guess so," added the other. "Imagine, if you please, Nick trying to call on any young lady at present. She'd be apt to have a swooning spell. For a time Buster will have to cut out all thoughts of girls' society. He can thank his lucky stars that his chums allow him to hang around."

"Have you had any lunch?" asked Jack.

"I think there's the rest of the bunch coming along the stone walk by the canal, right now. Perhaps we'd better postpone our little ride down the rapids until we get a bite. Buster will be starved."

"There he is dogging the footsteps of the rest," remarked Jack. "Herb is being cruel to the poor old chap. He won't let him join them. I guess he's suffered about enough by now, and we'll have to let up on it."

"Sure we will," agreed impulsive George. "Anyhow, we wouldn't have the nerve to make Buster take a canoe by himself, and shoot the rapids. Let's start out and join them. Perhaps Buster had discovered a good feed place, in his wanderings about the town."

"Ten to one he's noticed a dozen; and perhaps had a few bites before now," and Jack led the way across the little bridge connecting the island where the hatchery was situated, with the main shore.

Nick gladly admitted that he had marked a promising restaurant during his foraging expedition in search of the suit of clothes, which he had taken to the boat and donned.

"It ain't a tony place, fellows," he argued; "but considering the circumstances, er—I thought we wouldn't care for style."

"Why, no, not just at present, Buster;" George said. "You've got a level head for once. We're going to forgive you now, and restore you to good standing, on condition that you never, never again try to stock the camp with a menagerie of strange animals."

Nick promptly held up his right hand.

"I give you my word, boys, and thank you. Please overlook any slight association between myself and our recent invasion of Canada. And now come along. I tell you I feel as if I could clean out all the restaurants in the Soo. I only took a light breakfast you know, because of low spirits."

Josh held up both hands in despair, though he said not a word. There are times when silence is much more suggestive than any flow of language; and every one understood.

An hour or so later, before half-past two, they were on the little beach, talking with a couple of wiry-looking men, who claimed to be sons of the famous old guide of the rapids, John Boucher, who died a few years ago, after having carried thousands and thousands of summer tourists in his canoe through those swirling rapids, without ever a disaster.

Then the entire bunch of six boys took their places in the big and staunch canoe, with a wielder of the paddle at either end. Jack happened to occupy a position near the man in the stern, whose post is always the more important, since he guides the destinies of the swiftly running craft, while the one in the bow fends off from impending rocks.

Jack had taken this position more to observe how the experience affected his chums than for any other reason. He certainly never once dreamed that there might be a Providence in such a small thing as his choice of position.

Then began the first stage of the run, with the two Indians pushing the laden craft upstream by means of stout poles. They kept close to the shore, finding a way around the numerous rocks, and other obstacles, where the water boiled madly; and by slow degrees approached the railway bridge, under which the start is generally made.

"Ain't this simply glorious?" demanded Herb, as they found themselves surrounded by the churning waters, and gradually leaving the shore farther away.

"Wait!" said George, "if you think this is fine, what will you have to say when we get to running the rapids in fact? I've been through some smaller than these, and can guess how it feels."

"My! I'd like to keep doing it all day!" remarked Nick, feeling something like himself again, since he had been restored to favor once more.

"Well, at the rate of fifty per, your bank account would soon collapse. Besides, they say that the excitement is bad on fat people, so that they lose weight right along," George observed.

"You're joshing me, I know, George," declared the other. "If I believed you, I'd be tempted to stay over here while you fellows went on, and keep going all day, so I could cut off, say about thirty pounds or so. No, I wouldn't either; I forgot!"

"Yes, I should think you did forget Sallie," jeered Herb. "If you got out of her class she'd never forgive you, Buster. Besides, perhaps she wouldn't even see you if you wasted away to a shadow. Better leave well enough alone, and enjoy the good things of life."

"Here we go now; they're heading straight out on to the river!" cried Josh, as he nervously clutched the side of the big canoe near him; for they were seated two and two, with Jack just behind and George in front, as the boat narrowed.

The Indian guides were indeed pushing strenuously now, and when the water deepened both of them dropped their poles in the bottom of the canoe, to seize upon stout paddles and wield them furiously.

It was intended to reach a certain point in the river before turning the prow of the craft down toward the head of the rapids.

Long familiarity, every day in the week during the season, and many times a day, had made every rock and swirl known to these men. But although they knew the main channel like a book, seldom did any crew dare venture as close to the terrible jaws of the whirlpool as the veteran guide of the rapids, Old John Boucher, had always made it a practice of taking his parties.

Jack had looked several times at the man in the stern. Somehow, he did not wholly like his appearance. There was something about him to signify that he must have recently arisen from a sick bed. Perhaps, tempted by an influx of tourists, and the demand for experienced guides to take them through the rapids, he had come back to work a bit too soon!

"He doesn't seem as strong as the others," Jack was thinking, even as he turned his head from time to time as if to see what lay behind, while they were pushing up the sturdy current. "I can hear him pant as if short of breath. Goodness! I hope now nothing is going to happen to him while we're spinning along down through these old rapids. They say that whirlpool would swallow up anything; and that Old John was the only man whoever went into it, and came out alive. Whew!"

But Jack did not whisper these fears to his comrades. It was too late to change steersman now; and why spoil all their pleasure?

After all, no doubt there was not so much strength needed once they began to move swiftly along with the current, going half a mile in a couple of minutes, they had been told, though Jack doubted the accuracy of that statement at first.

Apparently the guides had overshot the mark at which they aimed; for as the canoe was turned, in the shadow of the bridge, Jack saw that the man in the bow glanced apprehensively over his shoulder while he knelt there, and immediately began to paddle furiously, as though trying to bring the boat back a little toward the American shore.

Had they gone too far, and were they speeding down in the track taken by the one daring prince of guides—a course that would actually skirt the verge of that whirlpool, of which such terrible things were said?

Jack shut his teeth hard at the thought. Then he gave himself up to the keen enjoyment of that glorious ride, when the canoe was seized upon as by invisible hands, and borne along at lightning speed.

Looking at the water alongside, foam-specked as it was, one could not believe the boat was moving at all, because both kept company. But all that was needed was for the voyager to raise his eyes, and send a look toward the shore, when he must realize the tremendous rapidity with which his frail craft was being carried along.

Things just seemed to fairly flit past, as though they were aboard a fast railway train. The boys were evidently enjoying the novel experience to the full, for their heads were constantly turning from side to side, and all seemed to be talking at once.

Jack was nervously looking ahead and on the left, for he knew they must now be approaching the whirlpool, where the eddying waters went furiously round and round and the center seemed to be a deep hole, like the dent a gigantic top would make in the mud.

Yes, there it was beyond, and they were speeding down at a pace that made one dizzy to notice it. He could feel that both Indian guides were paddling desperately away from the left, as though fearing that they were too close to the verge of that death chasm!

What if a paddle chanced to break right then and there? They carried spare ones fortunately—Jack had noted that; but all the same he hoped nothing of the sort would come about.

Hardly had this chilly idea flashed into Jack's mind than he heard what seemed to be a groan close to his ear. At the same time he felt the boat quiver in a suspicious manner. Turning instantly the boy was horrified to see that the Indian guide in the rear had crumpled in his place, with his head fallen forward, and seemed to be gasping for breath.

He had collapsed just at the most dreadful moment, when the canoe was swooping down close to the edge of the whirlpool!

CHAPTER XII

WINNING AN INDIAN'S ADMIRATION

Fortunately for all of them, Jack Stormways was not given to fear. In emergencies he acted from intuition, rather than through thinking things out, no matter however speedily.

There may come times when a second counts for everything. Jack believed such an occasion was now upon them; and he acted instantly.

The man in falling forward had pushed his paddle alongside Jack. It was as plain an invitation to fill his place as could have been given.

Making one swoop the boy snatched up the stout blade, and instantly dipped it over the port side. Desperately he exerted his strength to steer the canoe away from the fatal eddies that sought to draw them still further into the vortex.

The Indian in the bow may have suspected something of what had occurred; but he dared not turn his head now, or take his attention away from the rocks ahead for even one lone second.

As for the five boys, they were all staring at the near-by whirlpool as though actually fascinated by its terrors; and not suspecting how close they were to plunging straight into its grip.

With every atom of his strength did Jack work, dipping as deeply as he could, and striving against the giant power of the mill race on which they were speeding.

The edge of the circling current was horribly close; in fact they seemed to skirt its very border, closer perhaps than even the veteran guide ever carried his cargoes of tourists, when in his prime.

Jack fairly held his breath as the crisis came. He did not know, could not tell whether they would win out or not. It was an experience that would doubtless continue to haunt the lad for a long time. Perhaps he would awaken in the night with a start and a low cry, having dreamed that once again he sat in the canoe with the dark skinned steersman fallen in a faint, and the hungry maw of the whirlpool yawning so very close on their left that one could have tossed a chip directly into it.

"Wow! wasn't that a close shave though, boys?" shouted George, half turning his head to look at his mates; and then following his words with another cry: "Look at Jack, would you? Great governor! what happened?"

And as the others twisted around to look, they were amazed to discover that Jack was wielding that paddle like a veteran, his face as white as chalk, and his eyes staring; but his teeth firmly pressed together, with a look of grim determination on his young face.

Not a word was spoken until they had passed the last bristling rock, and spun out below where the foamy water took on a less violent aspect.

Then Bedlam broke loose.

"Sit still, all of you!" cried Jack, as he saw a movement on the part of his chums to get up; "you'll upset the canoe yet, if you try that. Wait till we reach the shore, and you'll know about it. The man has fainted, that's all; and I had to take his place."

"But he was all right when we started, for I looked around and saw him," declared Herb.

"That's true," Jack answered. "He keeled over just before we got to the whirlpool, and as he dropped his paddle right beside me, all I had to do was to dip it in, and exert myself a little."

"A little!" echoed George, with thrilling emphasis, "look at the beads of sweat on his forehead, fellows! Jack, honest now, you must have saved all our lives. Ugh! just to think, if the boat had swerved then, where would we be right now?"

They looked at each other, and turned paler than when passing through the yeasty waters of the rapids. But Jack tried to make light of it all.

"Oh! shucks!" he laughed, though his voice trembled a bit in spite of his wonderful nerve; "any of you would have done the same thing. Why, there was nothing else to do, to tell the truth."

"Me?" exclaimed Nick; "I'd sure have been so frozen with horror that all I could do would have been to grab hold of the boat, and shut my eyes. Kept 'em shut part of the time, anyhow. Felt like I had an awful temptation to just jump out of the boat, and into that nice water that was singing and gurgling along beside us."

"I guess you'd better never try the rapids any more then, Buster," said George, "if that's the way it affected you. I remember now hearing you say you never was able to walk on the ties of a railroad bridge, or look over a precipice, because something made you dizzy."

They reached the shore near the small house where Old John Boucher and his family, one of the sons said to be a preacher, lived in the days gone by. When the boys climbed out of the canoe, the Indian stepped in to help his comrade, who had by then come out of his swoon, and was able to feebly walk.

To the surprise of Jack the Indian who had been in the bow stopped to hold out his hard-skinned hand, and squeeze that of the boy.

"You Jack all right! Think it all over with everybody when Jim he fall. But you do right, think. Bully!" was what he said.

"Hurray!" shouted Nick, waving his new hat wildly.

"Three cheers and a tiger for our commodore!" exclaimed George; and they were given with a vim that caused many on the stone walk along the canal embankment to look down in wonder toward the little group.

Nor would the guide accept any pay for the trip. They could not force it on him.

"You ride with me all time, and not cent pay, Jack!" he declared, his black eyes sparkling with sincere admiration as he looked in the face of the white boy.

Of course the voyagers had lots to talk about while they continued their exploration of the city on the great canal. They even climbed the hill near where the government barracks stood during the Spanish-American war, and obtained a fine view of the entire neighborhood. Yet nothing attracted their attention as did the ever rushing rapids, where the waters of the greatest inland sea in the world emptied into the river that was to bear them through the other lakes in the chain, and by way of the St. Lawrence River, to the far-distant sea.

The thrilling adventure had apparently sobered the boys too, for there was much less horse play than usual, nor were jokes in order for the balance of that day.

Having some time to spare they took the ferryboat, and crossed to the Canadian side of the river below the rapids. Here they viewed the other canal, through which considerable commerce also passes, principally Canadian.

They also took advantage of their "visit abroad," as George called it, to inspect the big pulp mills, where spruce logs were ground up, and made into sheets that would later on become paper.

The latter end of the day was put in securing provisions calculated to last for a week or more, since they could not tell when another chance to procure supplies might come their way, once they embarked upon the bosom of Lake Superior.

Nick was once more in his element. He suggested all sorts of things that he had read about in his cook book. Had they sent him forth, with plenty of money and unlimited assurance, the chances were, as George declared, the expedition would have had to hire another boat, just to transport the stuff that fellow would have flooded them with.

"I bet he'd buy out a whole grocery store, given half a chance," said Josh.

"Why, we've got all the stuff right now we can stow away comfortably," declared Herb, scratching his head as he contemplated the numerous packages, and then looking toward his boat near by.

"Do as we suggested before, Herb," said Josh.

"What was that?" demanded Nick, suspiciously.

"Make Buster take up his quarters in the dinky. It'll be a ride that might take the shine off even that dash down the rapids."

"Not any," asserted the fat boy strenuously. "I'm too heavy for such monkey shines. Josh likes the water better than I do. You all saw how he can dive so gracefully just as if he had taken lessons from a granddaddy frog. If anybody has to be quartered in a dinky to make room, he's the chap, all right."

But after a while the last package was put away, and places found for all.

George drew Jack aside as the others were arranging things aboard the various boats.

"I've been making a few inquiries as to whether another small motor boat went through here," he remarked.

"Oh! yes, I'd come near forgetting Clarence," laughed Jack. "And I suppose he took the canal several days ago. He must have gained on us while we were losing time, stuck in the mud, stormbound and such things."

"Well, he didn't go through here, anyhow," replied George. "And the chances are ten to one he'd never think of using the Canadian locks."

"But he had a good start of us," remarked his chum.

"Well, do you think the Wireless is bound to monopolize all the mud in the St. Mary's river?" exclaimed George, indignantly. "I guess Clarence has stuck somewhere on the way up; and as he didn't have any bully chums to pull him off he's there yet!"

"We didn't see anything of him," mused Jack; "but then, there were lots of times when we had a choice of channels. Even the big boats take one of two that are buoyed and targeted. Yes, Clarence might have chosen one we let alone. But of course, if he hasn't passed through the canal, he must still be below."

"I'm sorry," George remarked, gloomily.

"I suppose so, because you're only thinking of that grand race you expected to pull off with your old rival, sooner or later. But the less I see of Clarence the better I'm pleased."

"Do we go ashore to a restaurant tonight, Jack?" continued the other.

"Let the others decide," Jack replied. "As for me, I think it would be the best thing to do. Josh is being overworked, as it is, and needs a little rest. Besides, Buster will be tickled, because that would leave more grub in the bunch for the future."

Little Jocko, the monkey, had made himself quite at home with the boys. They took turns having him aboard, and he furnished considerable fun for the crowd with his antics. As yet he had not become quite reconciled to Nick, and always showed his white teeth whenever the fat boy came around. But by treating him to choice bits of food Buster was winning the little chap over by degrees.

The balance were of the same mind as Jack when the proposition was put up to them. And accordingly they went to dinner in two detachments, Nick being with the first, and serving as a connecting link between both; for he was still there when Jack, Jimmie and George arrived at the eatinghouse; and sat them out in the bargain.

Still, the second squad had enough, and could not complain that Nick had made a famine in that particular restaurant; which Josh had hinted was possible, when telling them how the fat boy had refused to leave when they did.

It was an entirely different night they spent there at the Soo, from most of the quiet ones of the trip. Much noise continued throughout the livelong night; for the lock is lighted by electricity, and vessels can keep passing up and down the nineteen feet rise and fall at any and all hours.

Frequently during the night the hoarse whistle of some big steamer, or a tug towing whaleback barges, would sound close at hand, awakening those who were not accustomed to this bustling nature of things.

In the morning all of them declared that they had passed an uneasy night; and professed to be delighted because it would not be repeated.

"Tonight we hope to be in camp somewhere along the quiet shore of the Big Lake," said George, yawning and stretching.

"Yes," added Jack, with kindling eyes, "where those whoppers of speckled beauties are to be found, if looked for."

"Yum! yum! speed the hour!" mumbled Nick; and of course no one needed to be told that already his thoughts were turning to the glowing camp fire, and the tempting odors that would arise when the coffee pot was on, and the pink trout sputtering in the several fryingpans.

And shortly afterward, breakfast having been eaten at the same restaurant, which had evidently laid in a new lot of supplies since their last raid, they entered the big lock, to have the boats elevated to the upper level.

CHAPTER XIII

THE GREAT INLAND SEA

It was just ten o'clock when the trio of little motor boats started out of the canal, and headed for the open lake far beyond. Long afterward they could look back, and see the stone electricity building between the two locks of the canal; and in imagination the picture as viewed from its top would haunt them, with the churning rapids occupying the center of the scene.

Leaving the canal at its juncture with the river, they were soon in the neck of the lake. Far as the eye could reach, and many times farther, stretched the sparkling water, as clear as crystal; and cold enough to satisfy any one, even on as hot a day as this August one promised to be.

At noon they found a good chance to go ashore. Nick of course was solemnly warned that this was sacred Canadian soil, and that on no account was he to try and purloin any strangely marked animals he might discover prowling around.

"You know they have some queer beasts in these foreign lands, Buster," George remarked, shaking a finger before the other's stubby nose. "And make up your mind right now that you're going to let 'em all severely alone. Some time you can join an expedition sent out to Africa, to scoop up all sorts of freak cats and sich; but while you're with us we'd rather you restrained that curiosity of yours. It's going to get you in trouble, some fine day, Buster, you hear me?"

"That'll do for you, George. Just wait, and see if I don't have a chance to get back on you yet," replied the other, complacently. "But would you look at Josh, what he's bringing ashore now? Fish, as sure as you live. Bully for Josh! White fish, too, the best that grow in these waters, barring none. Tell us, where did you catch 'em, Josh?"

"With a silver hook, and from one of the Indian guides," replied the cook. "He netted 'em in the rapids, I guess. Heard that earlier in the season they get tons and tons of fish that way; two men in a boat, one in the bow to use the net, and the other to hold the canoe against the current with a pole. Bet you they'll eat fine, too."

"I'll help you clean 'em, Josh," volunteered Nick.

"All right, then; get busy, Buster. Anyhow, you know a good thing when you see it," returned the cook, only too willing to hand over the disagreeable task.

"Well," remarked George, as he and Jack lay there in the shade, waiting for the lunch call; "We're well on our way to the Agawa river region. Think we'll make it today, commodore?"

"I'm afraid not," replied Jack. "In the first place it looks dubious over yonder, as though we might get one of these famous Lake Superior storms you read about. If that drops in on us, we wouldn't like to be caught out on the open, you know, George."

"Well, excuse me, if you please," returned the other, with a shrug of his shoulders that spoke louder than his words. "Storms and my speed boat don't seem to agree very well. When one comes hustling along I prefer to be behind some sort of shelter, where I can laugh at the wind and the waves. But you spoke as if there might be still another reason for our not getting to the river tonight?"

"There is," Jack answered. "This time you may have the laugh on Herb."

"Say, you don't mean to tell me that the staunch old engine in the Comfort has been up to any antics?" exclaimed George; not without a touch of exultation in his voice; for Herb had jeered at him so many times, on account of his troubles, it was only natural that he should feel a little gratification to know there were others.

"Yes, it developed after we left the Soo," Jack went on. "Just like these mean things always do, you know. He's been limping along for the last half hour. Of course there's no telling how serious it may be. Let's hope we can fix it in short order. Some of us had better get at it right after lunch."

"If anybody can put it in apple pie order I guess you can, Jack," George said; "and if you need any help call on me, because you know Herb isn't much of a mechanic."

"That's kind of you, George," said Herb, who happened to be coming over to where the two were talking at the time. "That's the best thing about the motor boat boys; they like to josh each other, and get lots of fun out of things; but when it comes right down to trouble there isn't one of them who wouldn't do everything in his power to help a chum."

The call to eat caused them to make haste to gather around. In fact, there was always an involuntary sort of race to the mess table when the meals were eaten on shore, so that all partook. On this very day Josh noticed this fact particularly and made mention of it.

"Say, do you know you fellows are that prompt you just seem to jump into your places?" he said. "I start to pound a fryingpan with my big spoon, and before I get in five licks all of you are in a ring waiting for grub."

"Huh!" grunted George, "nothing funny about that. We have to!"

Nick of course took that as a reflection on him, and bridled up at once.

"That's unkind of you, George," he protested. "I was never known to take any fellow's share. An equal division is my rule always. And if some one chooses to decline a portion of his prog; and my appetite is not satisfied, what harm in commandeering the remains?"

"Oh! you're all right, Pudding; George is only tapping you as he does us all, when he gets the chance," Herb said.

"Well, I take my punishment decently, when my turn comes, don't I?" demanded George, as he received a generous portion of a delicious white fish, which had been rolled in egg, and cracker crumbs, and then cooked and browned in the grease from some salt pork placed in hot pans until it fried out.

"Sure you do;" Jack laughingly remarked. "And now forget all your troubles, fellows, and get down to work. Look out for bones. I've eaten white fish plenty of times, and they say they're never so good unless cooked right where they're caught."

"I believe it too," Josh continued. "Just like the pompano an uncle of mine used to tell us he caught down in Florida—used to jump in the boat, he said; and as they're a delicate, white-flesh fish like this, putting them on ice a week or so takes the flavor out. It also makes them crumble up when cooked."

"How is it, Buster?" Herb asked; but Nick only rolled his eyes, and kept on munching as though the fate of nations depended on his ability to clear off his tin platter within a given time.

When Nick was eating he wasted mighty little breath in talking, leaving all of that for more convenient times. Besides, he had a perfect horror of some time getting a fish bone in his throat.

"Wouldn't matter much with a lanky fellow like Josh, you see," he once said, in commenting on this fear; "because anybody could stick his fist down, and yank the fish-bone out; but my neck is so fat I'd choke to death long before you could say Jack Robinson. So don't bother me when I'm eating fish, please."

Afterwards Jack and George took a look at the engine of the Comfort. After doing a little tinkering they announced that it would probably run fairly well during the afternoon; but before starting on another day's trip more would have to be done to it.

This was not very comforting to Herb; but he made the best of a bad bargain; and with light hearts the motor boys again started forth.

Jack kept an anxious eye on the southwestern sky. He did not altogether like the looks of things in that particular quarter, and was resolved that if they discovered a promising campsite in the afternoon, they could not afford to pass it by, if it afforded an offing for the boats.

That tremendous sea, stretching for several hundred miles away to the west, opened appalling possibilities in the way of a gale. The staunchest steamers that ever plied the fresh water seas would sometimes be as putty in the grasp of a summer storm; and what of the three puny mosquito craft that were as chips on the water?

At three o'clock Herb announced that his engine was getting worse instead of better. And about the same time a welcome hail from George, who was moving along in the van as usual, told that he had by the aid of his glasses sighted a shelter.

"Then it's us to go ashore," declared Jack; nor was any one sorry in their hearts; since a little while before a distant sound like thunder had been borne to their ears from the low-down patch of hovering clouds.

The retreat promised to be all the shelter they wanted, though it would hardly have answered for larger boats. Immediately all became as busy as beavers, the two tents being raised, and stoutly secured, so that any ordinary gale could not carry the canvas off like a balloon.

Jack had hardly finished his share of the work before he got out his rod, and busied himself in trying for trout; for he fancied that they were to be found in the clear waters near by this cove, where a limpid little stream emptied into the Great Lake.

Nick, they all noticed, stuck close to camp. It would have to be something very attractive that could induce him to wander far from his fireside, especially when the camp was pitched on Canadian soil, where they grew such queer kitties.

This time it was Jimmie who seemed destined to get into a peck of trouble. Jack always declared that there seemed to be an evil spirit forever hovering around their camp, looking for chances to accomplish his work; and let there appear the least kind of an opening, and he was ready to jump in.

Jimmie was not much of a hunter or fisherman, though able to do either on occasion. But he did have a little fancy for wild flowers, and liked to pry around on occasion, seeing what he could discover.

Now, at this late day in the season, he knew he was not apt to run across any of these pretty gems of the woods; but there seemed to be some sort of fascination about poking here and there examining a bunch of magnificent moss of a pattern he had never set eyes on before, measuring some giant ferns, and watching the antics of a family of squirrels. These had their home in an old hollow tree close by, and seemed filled with mild curiosity concerning the intruders on two legs that had taken up quarters so boldly adjoining the cove.

Herb and George were busily engaged with the balky engine, trying to find out just what ailed the thing, so that it could be remedied once and for all. In the end they felt positive that the blame could be located and effectually cured. At least it was to be hoped so; otherwise the Tramp would have to tow the larger boat back to the Soo, where the trouble could be abated at the hands of a machinist.

Josh, according to his custom, was pottering around the camp, making a better fireplace out of stones, at which he could carry out his part of the business with more comfort and dispatch. If they had been going to remain any length of time here, Josh would have constructed a "cooker" worth looking at; for he was an artist in this particular line.

Nick was apparently quite content to lie around, "getting up an appetite for the next meal," as Josh sarcastically remarked.

"Just as if that were at all necessary," was what the fat boy hurled back at him; and the argument was so clinching that Josh subsided on the spot; for no one had ever seen the time when Buster's appetite needed to be coaxed.

Nick's eyes finally alighted on the repeating gun which Jack had leaned against a tree at a point where it would be out of harm's way. Now, Nick himself had seldom fired a gun, though ambitious to become a sportsman; because, as he wisely observed, "if I happened to be left in the woods some time, think I want to starve to death, with a gun in my hands, and plenty of fat game all around me? Not much!"

And in that spirit he had picked up the Marlin; bringing it to his shoulder in a clumsy way, time after time, in order to get accustomed to the movement.

"Keep the muzzle turned the other way, Buster!" commanded Josh, noticing that he was working the pump action of the six-shot weapon, as if he liked to see the ejector send the shell flying out at one side.

"Guess I know enough for that Josh," grumbled Nick, but at the same time moving still farther around, so that the cook might lose his fears; for when a meal was being prepared the fat boy always handled Josh with gloves, as he frankly admitted.

It was just as he was sitting thus that a sudden scream rang through the neighboring woods, sounding so shrill and angry that every one started as though a bolt of lightning had fallen from the clear blue vault overhead right into their midst, and exploded there!

CHAPTER XIV

NICK WIPES OUT HIS DISGRACE

Everybody in the camp jumped up.

All eyes were turned toward the point from which this racket sprang; and it was a strange sight that immediately met their astonished eyes. Jimmie was jumping about as though he had accidentally stepped into a bee's nest, and was now engaged in a hand-to-hand fight with the entire swarm.

Nick happened to be in a position where he could see better than any of his companions. And he immediately discovered that the troubles of the Irish lad were not at all imaginary.

Something was leaping back and forth, now threatening to land on the shoulders of Jimmie, and then springing to the low limb of a tree, or it might be the ground.

Nick had never before set eyes on such a strange creature, yet he realized that it was a wild animal. His late unpleasant experience was of course still fresh in his mind; and his first suspicion may have been that this was another specimen of a Canadian pussy cat.

Whatever it was, Jimmie seemed to be having the time of his life fighting. True to his inherited instincts, the Irish lad had snatched up some sort of stick, to serve him as a shillalah. It was a stout bit of wood too, and he wielded it in a manner that proved him to be a "broth of a boy." Several times it landed with a resounding whack upon the flying body of his antagonist, and at each connection the unknown beast was hurled heavily backward.

But evidently the furious animal was grim and determined. Instead of being cowed by these temporary setbacks it only resumed the attack with added zeal; so that Jimmie had often to throw up his left arm in addition, to fend off his foe.

Now, Nick chanced to remember that at the very moment he was holding a gun in his hands. With one of his chums in grave peril it seemed to devolve upon him to engineer a rescue party.

"Come on, boys! Jimmie needs help!" he shouted, starting to run forward as well as his bulk admitted.

"Careful of that gun, Buster!" called Herb.

"Yes, don't shoot Jimmie instead!" added Josh.

"Hold your fire till you can get 'em separated!" supplemented George; who being a little farther away at the time, managed to bring up the rear.

In this way then the quartette started to the assistance of Jimmie, who was still whanging away with might and main. What with the loud shouts of the aroused Irish lad, the whoops of the runners, and the angry snarling of the enraged beast, one would think a menagerie must have broken loose in the neighborhood.

Just then George happened to get a good look at the beast as it jumped up on the limb, and whirling, crouched to make another leap.

"It's a wildcat!" he shouted as loud as he could. "Be careful, Nick! Don't you try to grab it now, on your life!"

Nick heard, but was too busy to think of replying. The cat had sprung again at the pugnacious Irish boy, to be met with another smart thump that landed with a loud thud, and sent the beast sprawling to the ground.

"Ye would, hey?" howled Jimmie in derision, though the blood was streaked upon his face, where the sharp claws of the beast had scratched him. "Thry for it again, plaze! And be the powers, ye'll foind Jimmie Brannagan at home whin ye knock at the dure. Come on, ye omadhaun! I'll soon knock all the breath out of the body of ye! Wow!"

The Canadian cat was a fighter. It looked it every inch, now that the defiant defense of the intruder had aroused its fury. Once more it sprang to the limb of the tree, as though recognizing that here it had a better chance to leap than from the ground.

"Now! Buster! But be careful! Keep back Jimmie!" shouted George.

The others held their very breath, for they saw that Nick had the Marlin repeater up at his bulky shoulder. Perhaps every one of them was mentally hoping that he would not shut his eyes while pulling the trigger; for a little swerve might bring Jimmie within range, and the result be disastrous at that short distance.

Bang!

Instantly a series of whoops broke forth, and every fellow started forward once more, as though meaning to be in at the death. George and Herb and Josh had each managed to possess himself of some sort of improvised weapon. The first had in his hand a hatchet which he had been using at the time; Josh was waving his favorite big spoon, with which he was wont to beat the summons to meals on a pan; and the skipper of the Comfort had picked up a billet of wood while passing the fire, which he now flourished eagerly above his head.

Nick himself stood there, struggling with the pump-gun. As usual with novices he could not work the mechanism; for in his excitement he was trying to fire without having ejected the used shell; and no self-respecting modern arm will stand for that sort of treatment.

Fortunately all around, no second shot was needed. The animal was kicking its last upon the ground, and emitting agonizing screams of anger and pain. Whether by accident or real accuracy of aim, Nick had apparently managed to send the contents of the shell where it counted.

Already Jimmie was indulging in what seemed to be a war dance, waving his stick, and singing. George was compelled to laugh just to see his antics, streaked as his freckled face was with smootches of his own gore.

"Ye done it, Buster, sure ye knocked the silly gossoon clane over!" he called. "'Tis a broth of a boy ye arre, and afther me own heart. Look at the baste, would ye? If he hasn't got tassels on his ears!"

"That's a fact!" declared George, now arriving to see the last kick of the animal on the ground, and note the unquenchable fury shown to the very end. "Why, I tell you what it is fellows. A Canadian lynx, that's what!"

"It does look different from my cat—er, that other animal," admitted Nick, as he cautiously advanced, evidently ready to beat a hasty retreat should he discover any need.

"I've heard of the missing links," spoke up Josh; "but we never lost any; so this critter couldn't belong to us."

"A good shot, Buster, old man!" declared George, bending down to see where the charge had struck the beast while crouching on the limb, and preparing for still another leap at Jimmie.

Nick swelled up with importance. Apparently this was one of the few occasions when he could assume an attitude, and receive congratulations. Usually it was just the other way; and like a wise fellow he believed in making hay while the sun shone.

"Oh! pretty fair, considering how quick I had to shoot!" he remarked, carelessly, as much as to say that, given a little more time, and he could have done better.

Jack now came running up, having of course heard all the row, and being consumed with curiosity to know its meaning.

"What is it?" he called, as he ran. "Another Canada pussy cat?"

"That's just what it is," replied George quickly.

"And is Buster at his old tricks again?" continued the other; at which Nick was compelled to grin amiably, knowing his hour of triumph was at hand.

"Buster was in the mix-up, all right," George went on; "only this time he happened to be at the other end of the gun. Buster has covered himself with immortal glory. We all must knuckle down to him after this as the great Nimrod; for he has just slain the Jabberwock. Looky here, Jack; what d'ye call that?"

"Well, I declare, a big Canada lynx!" cried the newcomer, recognizing the dead beast as soon as he saw its queer tasseled ears, and its ferocious whiskers.

"It tackled Jimmie here, and they were having a hot old argument of it, Jimmie pounding with his club, and the cat using its claws," Herb said, turning to the Irish boy, to see how badly he was wounded.

Jack became sympathetic at once, and anxious in the bargain.

"Only a few little scratches you say, Jimmie," he remarked. "That's true, they don't seem serious; but it's always dangerous to be marked with the claws of animals that live on carrion, like lions, grizzlies or wildcats. And I'm glad to say I've got something along for just such a case. Come on back to camp with me."

Jimmie, still protesting, did so; while the others, dragging the lynx, made Buster head the procession, while they sang: "Lo! the Conquering Hero Comes; Sound the Trumpets, Beat the Drums!" greatly to the delight of the fat boy.

When Jack applied the purple colored tincture from a small bottle to the wounds on Jimmie's face and hands, the Irish boy gave a whoop of pain.

"Sure, the rimedy is worse nor the disease!" he complained.

"That's all right," said Jack; "just stand the pain for a little. It's an insurance against blood poisoning. Many a hunter has lost his life from little cuts no worse than yours, when they were caused by the claws of a wild beast. My father would not let me come out unless I carried this."

"What is it, Jack?" asked Herb, curiously.

"A strong tincture of permanganate of potash," was the reply. "Just remember that, will you; and it's got to be powerful enough to hurt like fun; eh, Jimmie?"

"Indade it did, that," was the immediate response; while the Irish boy screwed up his good humored face in a knot.

Jack went back to his fishing, for he had already managed to take one pretty good specimen of the Lake Superior speckled trout that would have weighed nearly four pounds; and was eager for more.

All the while he sat there, employing every device he knew of to tempt the finny denizens of the depths to bite, he kept one eye to windward. That low bank of clouds interested him; for it seemed to presage a storm.

Since everything possible had been attended to in order to ward off any evil effects of a gale, Jack did not stop fishing until he had succeeded in catching a fine mess, that would please the heart of Buster.

Josh was preparing the fish as fast as they were caught. Indeed, he dispatched Nick several times to see if there were any more forthcoming; when the sportsman would toss ashore his latest catch, and the cook's assistant hurry back with the prize, his hungry eyes fairly glistening with anticipation.

Of course it was a royally good supper that followed. Josh cooked the trout in the same capable manner he had served the lake white fish; and every fellow declared they had never tasted anything more delicious.

Still, there was plenty for all, and to spare. Even Nick had to shut his eyes with a deep sigh, because he had reached the extreme limit of his capacity; and a pan of trout remained untouched.

The growling of the thunder now became more pronounced. Across the heavens the zigzag lightning shot, in a way that was as terrible as it was fascinating. Supper done, the boys clustered near the fire, talking, and watching the coming of the gale. Again and again had Jack and George gone around, to see that every tent peg was clinched in the ground.

"They're going to hold, unless the wind tears the blessed things to flinders!" Jack had announced; and at the same time he had seen to it that the boats were protected by the friendly point of land from the giant waves that would soon be sweeping in from the sea beyond.

Already were they rising in majestic grandeur that was awe inspiring. The storm was about to swoop down upon the shore line, and hurl the rising sea against the mighty rocky barrier, as it had done for countless ages past without success.

"Oh! ain't I just glad I'm not out there!" exclaimed Nick, as he shudderingly surveyed the darkening picture of warring elements.

"But look there, fellows; what d'ye call that?" cried Herb, as he pointed a quivering finger at some object that had suddenly come in sight from the east.

It was a little motor boat, wallowing in the rising sea, and doomed to certain destruction unless able to make shelter immediately. And with the waves dashing wildly against the rocks, those aboard would never see the small opening through which the motor boat boys had come to their present snug harbor!

"It's the Flash!" shouted Jack; "and unless we manage to show them the way in, it's good-bye to Clarence and Bully Joe! We must do it, fellows. Come on!"

CHAPTER XV

HELPING AN ENEMY

Jack kept his wits about him.

He had snatched up something as he ran to the very point where he might best be seen through the flying spray. It was the conch shell which, with its apex sawed off, made a horn or trumpet that could be heard a mile away, under even the most discouraging conditions.

Reaching the point for which he had been aiming Jack immediately started sending a hoarse blast out over that tumultuous sea. The others waved their hats, and made suggestive motions toward the small inlet, to show that a boat could enter the cove where the stream of water emptied into the Big Lake.

"They see us!" shrilled Nick, dancing up and down in his excitement; for in this moment all past animosity was forgotten, because human lives seemed in jeopardy—the lives of those who had gone to school, and played baseball with them, in the days that were past.

"Yes, they're waving their hands!" declared Herb.

"And now they put about!" George added. "Careful there, Clarence! You nearly keeled over then on your beam ends. That was a narrow squeak! I'd hate to have the poor old Flash meet such a fate, not to speak of her crew."

"It's all right now, fellows!" cried Jack. "They're heading for the inlet. Run over, and be ready to give any help needed. In times like this let's forget that Clarence and Joe have always been up against us. We're all Americans now; and we must stick together!"

"Bully talk!" said Josh, hastening after George and Jack, leaving Nick to amble along in the rear.

Clarence knew how to handle his boat with considerable skill; and once he drew close in, he was able to see how the ground lay. Those on shore also directed him as best they could; and the net result was that the Flash finally shot around the point, arriving in the little sheltered bay that a kind nature seemed to have provided for just such emergencies.

As Jack had more than once said, could they but look back hundreds of years, no doubt they would find that it had sheltered fleets of Indian canoes many a time, when the storm king rode the waves of the Great Lake.

When the Flash had been moored safely, her crew came ashore. Joe Brinker was looking a bit sullen, as though he did not much fancy the idea of accepting aid from these fellows, whom he had always looked upon as enemies. But Clarence walked straight up to Jack, holding out his hand.

"I say it's mighty decent of you, Stormways, to throw us a line this way," he declared, with considerable feeling. "I admit I was badly rattled, and thought we were in for a wreck. Neither of us glimpsed this opening here, and we'd sure have swept by, if you hadn't signalled. I'm sorry now I ever—"

"Let by-gones be forgotten while we're here, Clarence," spoke up Jack. "See, the storm is whooping things up out there now, and it's just as well you're not on the lake."

Clarence did look, and shuddered at what he saw; for it was not a pleasant spectacle, with the lightning flashes, and the heaving billows, seen through the flying spray that even reached them by the tents.

"Get busy, fellows!" George called. "Carry everything inside. Yes, take that pan of fish, and the coffee, Nick. I guess our callers are hungry, and will be glad of a bite. Quick now, for here she comes with a rush!"

Hardly had they found shelter, and the flaps of the tents been secured, when down the rain pelted, to the accompaniment of the most tremendous thunder crashes any of them had ever heard; while the fierce wind tried its best to tear the canvas shelters from over their heads.

But the work had been well done, and the tents stood, though wobbling more or less under the fierce onset of the wind.

Clarence and Joe had been taken in with Jack and George, while the other four occupied the second tent. Seated on the ground, the two newcomers proceeded to break their fast, and drink what remained of the coffee.

"Guess you wonder what kept us back so long?" remarked Clarence, after they had finished the meal, and while a little lull came in the tempest without.

Jack and George looked at each other and smiled.

"We might give a good think," remarked the latter; "seeing that I pushed the nose of my Wireless boat so hard into Mud Lake that it took an hour and more for the other two to pull me off."

"Huh! that's where you were lucky, then, George," continued the other. "We didn't have any chums to do the pulling act; and so we just had to flounder there for hours and hours. I reckon we must have spent the best part of two days sticking in the mud. Happened that nothing came along but some big steamers; and they wouldn't stop to help a poor little motor boat off."

"Well, how did you get away finally?" asked Jack, interested.

"Worked our way out of it by ourselves; and we're proud to tell it," Clarence proceeded. "I managed to climb up into a tree that hung over the boat, and threw down branches until we made a mattress that would bear our weight. Then we got out a block and tackle we carried, and fixed it in a way to get a strong pull. I kept the engine working for all she would go, while Joe bent to the tackle; and inch by inch we finally yanked the Flash out of her mud berth."

"Good for you!" remarked George, with real emphasis. "Looking back, there's always some satisfaction in remembering how you managed to get out of a bad hole by means of your own wits."

"All the same, we wished many times we had some chums handy, who would give us a pull," said Joe, whom the meal and hot coffee had put in a better humor.

All night long the storm raged on the lake. Any vessel that was so unlucky as to be caught out in it was to be pitied, or at least those aboard were. Morning saw its abatement; but the seas were beating wildly against the rock bound north shore and it was sheer folly for any one to dream of putting out while such a condition of affairs lasted.

So they concluded to make a day of it. Clarence for the first time in his life began to realize what fine fellows these motor boat chums really were; and how they stood ready to forget all the trouble that he and his crony had been only too willing to shower upon them in the past.

They talked of dozens of things, some of which were connected with their life in school at home, and others that bore upon the recent series of happenings on the St. Lawrence river.

"Looks like we wouldn't have any more bother with Clarence after this," said Josh to Herb, as they watched Jack and the other two doing something at the camp fire that afternoon, just as though the best of friends.

"I hope we won't," replied the other; "but you never can be sure of Clarence. He's tricky; and besides, impulsive. Just now he means to drop all enmity toward us; because we've fed him, and treated him white. But wait till something rubs him the other way. That's the time to see if the thing is more than skin deep."

During the midst of their conversation George purposely mentioned the name of Jonathan Fosdick.

"What; do you know the old apple grower, too?" demanded Clarence, looking surprised.

Of course Jack told how they had found the old man sick in his stable; and helped him to his house.

"And he told us all about his runaway boy, Andy, too; and how word came he was working in a fishing camp up along this shore," George went on.

"Yes, we promised that if we ran across the fellow we'd tell him he was wanted at home the worst kind," Clarence remarked.

"And he was that thankful he just loaded us down with stuff—eggs, butter, and such. Couldn't do enough for us," Joe added, grinning at the recollection.

"History repeated itself then, for we promised the same thing," laughed Jack.

"And he just wouldn't take a cent in payment for the things we got," remarked George. "But see here, Clarence, it looks like we're in for another race between the Flash and the Wireless, to see which can get to the mouth of the Agawa first; for I hear there's a big fish camp there, run by a man at the Soo, where they take tons and tons of white fish, the trout not being for sale."

"I guess I get the notion that's struck you, George; and let me say right here, I still believe the Flash to be the better boat," Clarence went on, stubbornly.

"Shall we try it out then, tomorrow, when we leave here; in a friendly way of course, I mean?" George asked, eagerly.

"Take him up, Clarry!" said Joe.

"All right then, we'll call it a go," declared the other. "Only I wish we had something worth making a run for, a prize of some sort."

"It will give me some pleasure to be the one to tell Andy Fosdick that he's wanted bad at home," George observed.

"Then we'll call it a go; and this time you'd better look out for yourself, because the Flash has had a knot an hour added to her speed since we raced last. And besides, I didn't have any heart in that trial of speed, you know. That smuggler was forcing me to run my boat, to get him out of a pickle; and for me to win only meant that my boat would be lost to me. I was really glad to play him a trick in the end, and throw the race."

Jack and George may have had their own opinions with regard to the truth of the matter; but they knew enough to keep their tongues still. While the dove of peace hovered over the camp, it would be folly to stir these fellows up again.

Overhead the sun shone in a clear sky. Only for those waves the motor boat club could have easily continued on their cruise. But with the waning of the afternoon the seas began to sensibly decline.

"I prophesy a good day tomorrow for our race, George," Clarence remarked, as, in company with the others he sat by the fire, enjoying a feast that Josh and his assistants, Nick and Jimmie, had prepared for the crowd.

Jack and George were both of the same opinion since all the well known signs seemed to point that way. They sat up until a reasonable hour, chatting and singing; and Clarence realized as never before what a fine thing he and Joe were missing in never having found a chance to join this merry group before.

The night was a peaceful one. At early dawn the camp was astir, for much had to be done ere they might put out on the calm lake.

"Looks like a big mirror; didn't I tell you that wind had blown itself out?" remarked Clarence, upon casting his first glance beyond the point.

At eight they were all ready to leave the snug harbor that had opened so opportunely for the storm threatened crew of the Flash.

Clarence had charts also, and doubtless studied them eagerly when he had an opportunity to go aboard his boat again. For although this was only a friendly race, he always threw himself into whatever he did with a vim, heart and soul, that made defeat all the more bitter, should it come.

Of course Jack, deep down in his heart, knew full well that this was only a temporary truce in the warfare that had always existed between himself and Clarence. Once away from their society the other would soon drift back to his old way of thinking and acting. But Jack decided that not because of any unfriendly act on the part of himself or chums should these two find cause for again digging up the buried hatchet.

Leaving the cove, the four boats were soon moving along the glassy surface of the calm lake, headed almost due west. Somewhere, many miles away, lay the first goal, the mouth of the Agawa, which was to mark the expiration of the race.

"Ready, both of you?" demanded Jack, as the two rival speed boats ranged alongside the Tramp, one on either quarter.

"Ready here!" answered Clarence, briskly.

"Same here, Jack!" called George, hovering over his engine, which was running at about its next to slowest notch.

"Then go!" shouted the starter; and instantly both craft shot forward like arrows, while the rattle of their exhausts sounded as if a battle were in progress.

CHAPTER XVI

"WIRELESS DAY"

"Hurrah!" shouted Josh, wildly excited, and glad for once to be on the narrow speed boat.

"May the best one win!" called Jack, as he watched the rivals drawing ahead of the two slower boats.

"That means us!" laughed Bully Joe.

"Just wait and see!" answered Josh; between whom and Joe there had always been more or less bad blood.

Herb had given his staunch engine all it could stand; and as the Tramp stood by him, they were soon left far in the lurch.

"Talk to me about speed," observed Herb, as Jack turned his face that way, "strikes me the Wireless has her work cut out for today, to beat Clarence."

"You heard what he said about the improvement made when at the machinist's. It was a knot an hour increase, I believe," Jack remarked, casting a look down at the throbbing motor of the Tramp.

"That's right," Herb spoke up. "But you know we did some tinkering to George's engine, and he has always said that it ran better afterwards. Anyhow, it looks like a pretty race."

"I think so with you, Herb," Jack admitted. "Judging from here, they're running neck and neck now."

"Yes," continued the other, "but don't forget that tricky Clarence is always up to something. Two to one he's got a bit more speed held in reserve."

"Well, George knows him like a book," laughed Jack. "And make up your mind he'll keep something held back himself. Don't you remember he did before? Possibly Clarence may be the one to run up against a surprise after a while."

As the racers drew farther and farther away, those in the other boats began to think of other things. None of them had half the interest in the outcome of the rivalry as did George. With him there were many old accounts to square; and he meant to make a good job of it, if he had his way about the matter.

For some miles the two speedy motor boats kept along, neither appearing to gain half a length on the other. If one seemed to be going ahead, the skipper immediately busied himself stopping the advantage. It was as if both were holding themselves in for the home stretch.

Josh was on needles and pins all this while. He paid little attention to what lay in the rear. Part of his time was taken up in scanning the watery waste ahead, through the powerful marine glasses. And when not thus employed he sat there, quivering with suspense, wondering whether there would come a sudden stoppage of the engine, which might spring from one of its eccentric tantrums.

But, strange to say, the motor seemed to be doing its best today, as if bent on meriting all the good things its builders had said in their catalogue.

"I see it!" suddenly hoarsely whispered Josh, in a mysterious way, as though he did not wish those in the other craft to overhear him.

"You mean the little bay at the mouth of the river?" queried George, setting his teeth hard together; for he knew that the crisis so long awaited was at hand.

"Sure, look for yourself, George," handing him the glasses.

"Yes, I believe you're right," returned the skipper of the Wireless, as he once more turned his attention to his engine. "Now, get in the middle of the boat, Josh, and don't move any more than you can help."

"You're going to open up, then?" asked the tall, ungainly lad, feverishly.

"I am. Are you ready?" George went on.

"My hair is parted exactly in the middle, I believe," chuckled Josh. "You know Buster used to say that was one thing you made him do when he was on board here. Let her go, George! Get the jump on him; it may count in the end!"

A shout from Bully Joe was the first knowledge Clarence had that his rival had taken the bit in his teeth, and shot ahead. Instantly the speed of the Flash was increased; and the two powerful engines began to throb like little giants; while the sound of the exhausts, from which the mufflers had been entirely removed, was like the tattoo of a couple of snare drums calling the long roll.

Josh steadied himself as best he could; though when the boat was rushing through the water at this frightful speed it did not seem so cranky as when at rest.

"George, we're gaining on him!" he said, in a husky voice that trembled with the excitement under which Josh labored.

"I see we are; and still I could get a bit more out of old Wireless if hard pushed. Don't worry, Josh; we're bound to show Clarence up for a bluffer this time, sure."

"If only something don't happen!" gasped the anxious Josh, with an intake of breath that was like a big sigh.

"Make your mind easy on that score," said George, positively. "Nothing is going to break down. She's running as smooth as silk, and never missing a stroke. Oh! ain't this great, though? I've looked forward to this ever so long. Wouldn't I like to be close enough right now to see the look on Clarence's face."

"It's as long as a foot rule, I warrant you!" chuckled Josh. "Don't I know them two fellows though? They take a beat hard. Ten to one that if you are ahead when we come to the bay, they'll go on past, and never enter at all."

"Well, now, that wouldn't surprise me one little bit," remarked George.

Slowly but surely was the Flash falling behind, or rather the other boat forging ahead. Doubtless Clarence must be trying every device known to ambitious racing skippers in order to just coax a little more speed from his engine; but it was now keyed up to top-notch, and utterly incapable of doing a particle better.

Already Clarence must know that he was badly beaten, unless fortune stepped in to bring about an accident to the Wireless.

"That's what he's playing for now," said George, when his companion suggested this very thing. "But I reckon Clarence will find himself barking up the wrong tree. This race has just got to be mine. You hear me warble, Josh?"

It was not often George spouted slang; but the excitement had seized upon him to such an extent now, that he hardly did know what he was saying.

Minutes crept along.

Now the Flash was a stone's throw in the rear, and losing all the while.

"Careful about the turn, George," cautioned Josh, as they came near where the bay opened up. "We don't want to lose this thing at the last stretch. Now you're safe to turn in. Hurrah! hurrah! hurrah! siss! boom! crash! we win!"

The Wireless safely made the turn, and thus Josh announced her victory.

"What did I tell you," Josh went on. "Look at 'em, George! They're spinning on right past, and don't mean to come in at all. Clarence won't even look this way, but keeps staring ahead. Talk to me about taking a beat to heart, there never was a fellow as bad as Macklin, in baseball, hockey or any sport. Well, good-bye to you, fellows! Come again when you can't stay so long. It's Wireless day, you know!"

There was no answer to the shout with which Josh wound up his remarks. He saw Bully Joe wave his hand in a derisive way, and then the Flash passed by at full speed, as though the race were still on.

There was a big camp on the shore, and several boats drawn up on the beach. Many signs told that this was one of the favorite places along the north shore for the white fish men to gather. Doubtless innumerable barrels of this delicate inhabitant of the Great Lakes were shipped from this coast during each season; with the supply still undiminished.

It had been agreed upon that George was not to go ashore until the rest of the little motor boat fleet arrived. This was not for half an hour or so, since the Comfort was not capable of doing better than ten miles an hour, and the more speedy Tramp had to accommodate her pace to that of the steady boat.

Nick and the rest gave the victor a good cheer as they turned the point, and entered the bay at the mouth of the famous trout river.

Then the three craft made for the beach, off which they anchored, to go ashore in the smaller boats.

There were some shanties and tents in sight, with a number of rough looking men; who however seemed glad to welcome the boys. The smell of fish was everywhere, as was natural.

"Do you happen to have a young fellow here in this camp by the name of Andy Fosdick?" Jack asked a man who seemed to be the boss.

"Yes, but just now he's out at work. There's a boat coming in and p'raps Andy may be one of the crew," the other replied.

They waited until the boat landed, and those who were in it jumped out. Jack could use his judgment, and he immediately selected a sturdy looking young chap, with a skin the color of an Indian's, as the one they sought.

"Come along, fellows," he said to his chums; "and we'll find out."

He made straight for the young man; who, seeing the procession approaching, and all eyes glued eagerly on him, stood there looking curious, and a bit apprehensive, Jack thought.

"Are you Andrew Fosdick?" Jack asked, as they reached the spot where the other stood, one hand resting on the edge of the boat, from which his comrades were already shoveling their catch of fish.

"That's my name, though I generally answer to plain Andy," replied the fisherman wondering doubtless what all this meant, and why these boys should want to see him.

"Bully!" exclaimed Nick. "Found him the first shot! We're sure in great luck on this cruise, fellows!"

"Tell him what you want with him, Jack," urged Herb, who saw the other was being consumed with anxiety.

"We have come straight from your father, Andy," said Jack, softly. "He wants you to come home to him."

Then they saw a hard look pass over the dark face of Andy Fosdick.

"It ain't no use, boys," he said, bitterly. "He run me off long ago, and I don't go back there again. I'm gettin' to forget my name even is Fosdick, and that settles it."

CHAPTER XVII

CAUGHT NAPPING

Jack was shocked at the words and manner of the young fisherman. His chums even half turned away in disgust, believing that their mission was doomed to failure. But Jack did not give up a thing so easily.

"Wait," he said, quietly; "I don't believe you know, Andy. When did you hear from home last?"

"Never once," gritted the other, morosely, showing that his wrongs had eaten into his very soul. "Didn't want to, neither. Made up my mind I cud take care of myself. Done it too, all these years. Got money laid up; and goin' to be married in the fall."

"Then you didn't know your mother was dead?" Jack went on.

"Oh!" exclaimed Andy, starting, and showing signs of emotion. "I never heard that Ma was gone! Yes, I'm sorry I didn't see her again. She was never so bitter as dad; but only weak like."

Jack heard him sigh, and knew a start had been made.

"Listen, Andy," he went on; "your father is subject to strokes. One of them will carry him off. It may be today, or tomorrow, but not a great while can he stay here. He is bitterly sorry for what he did. He wants to tell you so, to ask you to forgive him before he too dies."

Andy's head fell on his broad chest, and Jack believed he saw his frame quiver with some sort of gathering emotion.

"He has made his will, and left you everything, Andy," he continued. "If you are to be married, that will be your home. He begged us to find you, to tell you all this; and that if you would only come back to forgive him, he would die happy. Won't you do that, Andy? Once he goes, the chance can never come to you again; and you're bound to feel mighty sorry as the years go by."

Nick nudged George, and whispered.

"Did you ever hear the beat of that, George? Ain't our Jack the born lawyer though? He ought to be in your dad's office, studying for the bar, that's what."

"Hold your horses, Buster!" answered the one addressed, eagerly waiting to see what effect Jack's logic might have upon Andy.

The struggle however was short. Presently the young fisherman glanced up; and as soon as he could see the look on his bronzed face Jack knew his case was won.

"I'll go back to the old man," he said, firmly. "I guess 'taint right he shud die and not have a chance to say what's on his mind. And thank ye for tellin' me."

"But when will you go?" Jack continued. "There is need of haste, because nobody can say just how long he may live."

"A boat'll be along this arternoon, and we ship some barrels on her. Guess the boss'll let me off when he larns the reason," Andy replied.

"If you like, I'll tell him the whole story?" Jack suggested.

And this he did a little later. He found the boss full of sympathy, rough man as he seemed to be. And Andy readily received permission to break the contract he had made for the season.

"Well, what's doing now?" queried Herb, as the bunch wandered around, observing the various interesting phases of the fishermen's business; for a boat was loading with barrels full of the catch, which were going direct to the Soo, from where they would be carried by express to Chicago, or other distributing points.

"Too late to go on today," said Jack. "Besides, I want to have a try with some of the big speckled trout that they tell me lie around here. They take plenty, but have to throw them back, or eat them, as the law does not allow any sale of trout. Think of a seven pounder on my rod."

"Well, get at it then, Jack," laughed George. "You'll never be happy till you do hook a monster. We'll promise to help you eat him, all right; eh, fellows?"

"All he can bring in, and then some," declared Nick; making his mouth move in a suggestive way that caused his mates to laugh.

"Be careful, Buster," warned Herb. "You know you said you meant to cut down on your grub. Instead of losing, you're gaining weight every day. If you keep on like that, Rosie won't know you when we get back home."

But Nick only grinned as he replied calmly: "Well, Rosie ain't the whole thing. There are others, perhaps."

"Listen to the traitor, would you?" exclaimed Josh. "Won't I tell on him, though, when we get back? I bet he's thinking right now of that cute little elephant, Sallie Bliss!"

"All right," admitted Nick, brazenly. "Who's got a better right, tell me? And even you admit that she is cute. Just mind your own business, Josh Purdue. The fact is, you're just green with envy because of my noble figure. Pity you couldn't have a little of my fat on your bones!"

"Noble figure!" exclaimed Josh, pretending to be near a fainting spell. "Shades of my ancestors, excuse me! I may be envious, but I ain't conceited, like some people, and that's the truth."

Jack left them in this sort of warm argument; but he knew that no matter what was said, Nick and Josh would not openly quarrel.

He asked numerous questions as to the most likely spots for the big trout; and having secured some bait, started into business. While thus employed he saw the steamer come along, and the boat loaded with barrels go out to meet her, as she stopped her engines.

"There's Andy stepping aboard, carrying his grip," Jack said to himself. "And I'm glad he proved so sensible. The old man will be wild to have him again. Yes, it was a lucky day for him in more ways than one when we started for his house to get a supply of butter, eggs and milk. Nick thought the luck was all on our side; but he can never see far beyond meal time."

As the afternoon grew on, and the steamer became hazy in the distance, Jack began to have some bites. And then came the thrilling moment when he found himself engaged with one of those famous monster speckled beauties for which this region is noted, and specimens of which he had seen in the breeding ponds of the Soo government fish hatchery.

It was a glorious fight, never to be forgotten; and at last Jack had his prize in his hands. Nor did the luck stop there. The fish were hungry, apparently; for in less than five minutes Number Two gave him even a harder struggle than the other victim; and in this case also Jack won out.

So they did have trout galore for supper; and even Nick was surfeited for once. All of the boys declared that they had never tasted anything finer than these big Lake Superior trout, freshly taken from the icy waters of the big reservoir, and cooked as only Josh Purdue could do it.

"Yum! yum!" Nick went on, after being actually pressed in vain to have another helping; "I'd like to stay right here for a month. Seems to me I'd never get tired of that pink flesh trout. Don't ever want to hear mention of a Mississippi catfish again after this."

"How about Canada kitties?" asked Herb, maliciously.

Nick declined to answer. That was a subject on which his comrades knew his mind full well; and he did not mean to argue it again.

Mutely he pointed to the skin of the lynx which had fallen to his gun, mutilated a little, to be sure, by the charge of shot that had been the means of its death; but worth its weight in silver to the fat Nimrod; and Herb closed up like a clam.

In the morning they prepared to go on again; though Herb and Jack had, when by themselves, seriously talked over the subject; and were beginning to arrive at the conclusion that this tremendous fresh water sea was hardly the best cruising ground for such small craft as the motor boats; and that they would be wise to cut short their former intention of reaching Duluth.

"Better keep an eye out for dirty weather, boys!" the boss of the camp had observed, when shaking hands as they said good-bye.

Nick could see no signs of anything ahead that looked like a storm; and he was inclined to believe the other must be wrong in his guess.

"Must be one of them old croakers we hear so much about," he remarked to Herb, as they went on along the coast of the Big Lake. "Always expecting things to happen that don't come to pass. I don't see any storm, do you?"

"Not a sign," replied the skipper of the Comfort; who was anxiously keeping tabs on his engine, as though he had reason to fear a repetition of the former trouble.

But in the end it proved to be George who brought the little expedition to a halt. After acting so splendidly in that fierce race with the Flash, lo and behold, the motor of the Wireless broke down during the early afternoon.

They tinkered at it for an hour and more, Jack coming over to take a hand; but apparently little progress was made. Jack was worried. They were too far away from the fish camp to think of towing the disabled boat back; and a harbor did not offer within reaching distance beyond.

The afternoon began to wane, and there seemed nothing for it but that the three motor boats should anchor just where they were, and pass the night on the open water. All would be well if the weather remained fair, and no strong southerly wind arose during the night. Jack did not like to think what might happen in case such a thing did come about.

So as night came on they made things as snug as possible, ate supper aboard, and determined to keep up their courage, in the belief that nothing would happen to alarm them.

But about an hour after midnight Jack, being on the watch, was thrilled to hear a sudden and entirely unexpected boom of thunder.

Instantly everybody was awake, and stirring; loud voices began to be heard, as the others thrust their heads out of the tarpaulin covers that served as boat tents when the crews slept aboard; and excitement reigned.

The very thing that Jack had dreaded most of all seemed on the verge of coming about; since they were caught on the open lake at night, with a storm threatening.

CHAPTER XVIII

A NIGHT OF ANXIETY

"Hey! here's Nick getting into his cork jacket already!" called Herb.

"All right," said the one in question, firmly. "Think I want to get washed out on that pond without something to hold me up? Remember, I'm a new beginner when it comes to swimming. And then I've got more to hold up than the rest of you."

"Well, help me get this tent down first," remonstrated Herb. "We don't want to be caught by a storm with these things up, you know."

"But it might rain?" Nick protested.

"Let it. We've got oilskins; and perhaps there'll be plenty of time left to get into the same. Take hold there."

Herb was right; and the crews of all the little motor boats had already started to stow away the big covers. Jack kept things as snug as possible aboard the Tramp, in case of a downpour; and that was not at all the thing he feared most.

They were within fifty feet of cruel looking rocks. If the wind broke out from any quarter that would send the big billows churning against that barrier, the fate of the motor boat fleet could be easily guessed.

In a little while everything had been done that seemed possible; after which they could only sit there, and await whatever was to be handed out to them.

Nick and Josh were plainly nervous; and even Jimmie showed some signs of apprehension, nor could they be blamed for this timidity.

"What if one of the boats is swept away?" suggested Josh; who, being in the narrow-beam Wireless understood that he had much less chance for safety than those who manned the other craft.

"No danger of that happening," Jack replied, quickly. "The only thing we have to fear is being smashed up against these rocks. Our boats would cave in like puff balls."

"That's what," Josh went on. "Perhaps fellows, we ought to go ashore in the dinkies while we have the chance. Even if we lost the boats we'd save our lives. And I promised my folk at home I wouldn't take any unnecessary risks, you know."

But George only sniffed at the idea.

"Rats!" he exclaimed. "There you go just as usual, magnifying the danger, Josh. As for me, I'm going to stick like glue to this old Wireless. Just see me deserting her because a little squall chances to blow up. Get ashore if you feel like it. And you too, Buster; only remember, if we should be blown miles away, you two fellows would be apt to starve to death in this lonely region."

"That settles it," said Nick, immediately.

If there was any chance of his starving, he stood ready to accept all sorts of perils rather than face that possibility. And doubtless George knew all this when he put the case so strenuously.

Josh too decided that he did not want to go ashore. If the others could stand the danger, he would too.

"It may not be so bad for us, fellows," observed Jack. "Because, if you look up, you'll see that the clouds are coming from the land side. And every bang of thunder up to now has been from that direction too. The storm this time doesn't mean to cross the lake, and hit this shore. And unless it changes around, we'll be protected from it by these very rocks we feared so much!"

"Bully! bully! Good for you, Jack!" cried Nick, as if greatly relieved. "I'm feeling so much better I almost believe my lost appetite is returning."

"Well, it's so, ain't it?" demanded the other.

"Sure it is," echoed Jimmie, with delight in his voice.

"That's the best news I've heard this long while," remarked George, who despite his seeming valor, was secretly much distressed over the outlook.

The thunder increased in violence. Then they heard the sweep of the wind through the pines and hemlocks on the shore. And in less than ten minutes the rain was pouring down like a deluge.

They had secured things so that little harm would be done. Still, the outlook was far from attractive, with several hours of darkness ahead; during which they must keep on constant guard, not knowing at what minute the wind might take a notion to veer around to some quarter, that would send the waves dashing against the rockbound shore so near by.

It seemed as severe a gale as the one they had experienced only a short time before. Indeed, Jack was of the opinion that the wind was even greater, though they did not feel it the same way, because of the shelter obtained from the land.

They would never be apt to forget that night, no matter how time passed. Watching was serious business for Nick; and three times he was known to creep over to where Herb kept his cracker bag, doubtless to interest himself in a little "snack," so as to briefly forget his other troubles.

Nor did Herb have the heart to take him to task about it. Their situation was so very distressing that he could think of nothing else. Every time the lightning flamed athwart the black sky the boys would look out at the troubled waters stretching as far as the eye could see; or else send an anxious glance toward the grim rocks that loomed up so very close over their bows.

Hours seemed like days. Nick groaned, and declared he ached in every bone.

"What d'ye think of me, then?" demanded Josh. "You're well padded; while I reckon my poor old bones are going to stick through, pretty soon. I dassent stand up, because George won't let me; and you can. I wish you had my berth, Buster."

But at last Herb declared that there were certainly signs of dawn coming in the east. Every eye was turned that way; and upon learning that the news was true the boys began to take on fresh hope.

"Well," George said for the tenth time, "I'm glad of one thing, and that is we managed to get my engine in working order last night before supper. Goodness knows what a fix I'd have been in otherwise, if we had to put out to sea when the wind changed."

"Oh! murdher! I hope it won't do the same!" exclaimed Jimmie, who overheard the remark, and was filled with dismay as he surveyed the wild scene that stretched away off toward the southern horizon.

"Can't we manage somehow to cook something warm?" asked George.

"Yes, that's it," immediately echoed Nick, beginning to bustle around in the steady old Comfort. "We'll all feel so much better if we have breakfast. Nothing like a full stomach to put bravery in a fellow, I tell you."

"Oh! how brave you must feel all the time, then!" observed Josh, sarcastically.

But Jack knew that this time the fat boy spoke the truth. When people are wet and shivering things are apt to look gloomy enough; but once warm them up, and let them eat a hot meal, and somehow a rosy tinge begins to paint the picture.

They knew just how to go about the matter; and those wonderful German Juwel kerosene gas stoves filled the bill to a dot; as Nick declared, after the delightful aroma of boiling coffee had begun to reach his eager nostrils.

And while the wind still howled through the pines up on the high rocks, and the billows rolled away toward the south, growing in size as they drew farther off shore, the motor boat boys sat down to a tasty breakfast.

"Now, this isn't so bad," observed Nick, as he started in on what had been dished out to him by Herb, who this time had done the cooking.

"It will be for the boss if he don't get to work in a hurry," Josh flung across the watery space that separated the boats.

"Don't worry on my account," laughed Herb. "I've got a mortgage on the balance in the fryingpan, and he'd better not touch it on his life."

"Think the bally old storm is over, Jack?" asked Nick, presently.

"The worst of it is, and I believe the wind seems to be dying down a little," came the ready reply, as Jack swept the heavens with anxious eyes.

"I thought that last gust came out a little more toward the west," remarked one of the others.

"I'd hate to know that," Jack said. "For old sailors say that when the wind backs up into the west, after being in the north, without going all the way around, it means a return of the storm, from another quarter."

"Time enough to get ashore yet!" muttered Josh.

"Go ahead, if you want to," George said grimly. "Take some grub along, if you make up your mind that way. But I don't stir out of this boat unless I'm thrown out. Understand that?"

An hour later, and Jack saw that his worst fears were realized.

"Wind's getting around fast now, fellows," he announced.

"It sure is," Herb admitted; for he had been noticing the increased roughness of the water for a little while back.

"What must we do, Jack?" asked George, with set teeth, and that look of determination in his eyes that stood for so much.

"Hold out as long as we can," came the reply in a steady voice. "Then, when the danger of our being dashed against the rocks grows too great, we'll just have to up-anchor, and start our engines to moving. It will be safer for us out yonder than so near the shore."

Another half hour went by. Then the little boats were pitching and tossing violently, as the full force of the onrushing waves caught them.

"Can't stand it much longer, Jack!" called out George, who was having the most serious time of all.

"Then we might as well make the move now as later!" called Jack. "So get going, both of you. And remember to stand by as close as you can, so that we may help in case an upset happens to any boat."

Of course George knew his chum had the cranky Wireless in mind when he said this; but the peril was not alone confined to the one boat.

Accordingly the engines were started, the anchors gotten aboard after a tremendous amount of hard work; and the little motor boat fleet put to sea, with the intention of trying to ride the storm out as best they might.

If the engines only continued faithful all might yet be well.

CHAPTER XIX

PERIL RIDES THE STORM WAVES

There were anxious hearts among the young cruisers as they started to leave the vicinity of the shore, and head out upon the big heaving seas.

So long as they could keep the boats' bows on the danger would not be so great as if they tried to turn; when those foam-crested waves would strike them sideways, and threaten to turn them on their beam-ends; which would mean destruction.

The motors sang like angry bees whenever the little propellers chanced to be exposed after a retreating wave had passed. This was where the greatest peril lay; for the strain on the engine and shaft was terrific at such times, owing to the rapid change of pace.

So Jack, Herb and George found themselves compelled to stick constantly at the job, manipulating the lever, so as to shut off power with each passing wave.

They did not make fast time away from the shore; but at the end of half an hour had reached a point where it seemed the height of folly to go farther.

"How is it, George?" Jack sang out.

"Everything moving smoothly over here so far," came the reply.

"And you, Herb?" continued the commodore of the fleet.

"No fault to find, only it's hard work; and I hope we don't have to keep it up all day," replied the skipper of the Comfort.

"I don't think that is going to happen," Jack observed. "Seems to me the wind is dying down. When that happens, the waves must gradually grow smaller. Perhaps by afternoon we may be able to proceed, and hunt for a harbor farther along."

"Well, now," George remarked. "I wouldn't be sorry any, let me tell you, fellows. I've been balancing here like a circus acrobat this blessed hour and more, till my legs are stiff."

"Think of me, would you!" bleated Nick.

"Shucks! you're like a ball, and nothing ought to hurt you!" declared Josh.

"I've got feelings, all right, though," the fat boy protested. "But I certain do hope we get our feet on solid ground right soon. I'd just love to see a fire going, and smell the hickory wood burning."

"Yes, it's something more than hickory wood you're longing to smell, and we all know it for a fact," Josh fired back at him.

Nevertheless, they one and all did find encouragement in what Jack had stated. The wind was certainly beginning to die out; and while as yet there could not be any appreciable difference noted in the size of the rollers upon which they mounted, to plunge into the abyss beyond, that would come in time.

During the morning that followed the boys who handled the engines of those three little power boats found occasion to bless the makers of the staunch motors that stood up so valiantly under this severe test.

They had taken on an additional supply of gasoline while at the Soo, and there was little danger of this giving out. Still, as Nick said, this energy was all wasted, and reminded him of soldiers "beating time."

Now and then the boys were able to exchange remarks, especially the three who were not kept busy during this time.

Jack listened to what was said, and while he made no attempt to break into the conversation, he gathered from it that at least Nick, Jimmie and Josh were about ready to call the westward cruise off, and turn around.

So he made up his mind that the matter must be threshed out the very next time they could gather around a fire on shore. As for himself, Jack was thinking along the same lines, and ready to go back to Mackinac Island's quiet waters, in the straits between Lakes Huron and Michigan.

Noon came along, to find them still buffeting the waves; but there had been a considerable change by then.

"After we've had a bite," called out Jack, at which Nick instantly showed attention; "I think we'd better make a start out of this. The waves you notice no longer break, and while your boat would roll more or less, George, I don't think you'd be in any great danger of turning turtle, do you?"

"Oh! I'm only too willing to put out," came the answer. "Anything but this horrible marking time. I like to see the chips fly when I use an axe. I want to see results. And here, this blessed little motor has been churning away for hours, without getting away from our old stand. Yes, let's eat and run."

"That would be bad for digestion," spoke up Nick. "I don't believe in hurrying over meals. I was warned against doing it, unless I wanted to waste away to skin and bones like Josh here."

"Oh! you can take as long as you like," said Herb; "only get busy now, and dish up anything you can find. There's some cold baked beans handy; and open some of that potted beef; it ought to be tasty with the crackers and cheese."

"I'm on the job right off," declared Nick. "You know you never have to hurry me about getting things to eat."

"Mebbe that's why your digestion is so good," said Herb, sarcastically; but the fat boy only grinned as he crawled back to where the eatables were kept.

Later on they did head more toward the west, and start moving through the swinging seas. Constant watchfulness became necessary, for there was always danger that in some unguarded moment one of the billows might roll a boat over like a chip.

So they kept going on, constantly varying their course to meet emergencies, and making progress along the coast. It was splendid manœuvring for the young pilots of the motor boats; though they rather thought they had had quite enough of it, and would be only too glad to call a halt.

Jack was watching the shore line ahead, whenever he could, in order to learn if a haven came in sight. He had Jimmie frequently use the glasses when they were on a wave crest; and kept hoping to hear him cry out that he believed he had sighted the harbor they hoped to make before night came on.

As the waves still further diminished in size, they were enabled to make better time, since they no longer feared an upset. Indeed, about the middle of the afternoon they ceased entirely to head the boats into any billow; and all of them declared that they felt proud of what had been accomplished.

"I say, Jack!" called out George, as the two boats happened to draw near each other.

"Well, what is it?" answered the one addressed, popping his head up.

"How does it come, d'ye suppose, that we haven't seen a blessed steamer all this morning, going in either direction?" George went on.

"Why," replied Jack. "Because they had warning from the weather bureau that a storm was coming, and delayed starting out. These captains know what it is to meet up with a Lake Superior storm."

"Yes," spoke up Jimmie, "it's only the nervy little boats like ours that laugh at all the blows as comes along. Look at us, would ye, smashin' through the big waves like the sassy things. Slap! bang! and come again, would ye? Sure, it's weather on'y fit for motor boats, it do be."

"Yes," laughed George, "we're all mighty brave about now; but I tell you boys, I felt squeamish for hours when the storm was on. I knew what would happen to us if the wind whipped around before morning. Excuse me from another experience like that. Wonder where Clarence and Joe were then?"

"That's so, they did go on," Jack remarked. "I hope they had shelter. I wouldn't want my worst enemy to be wrecked on such a terrible night."

A short time later Jimmie cried out again: "There do be a steamer comin' along there, Jack!"

"Steamer nothing!" echoed Josh, who happened to be using George's glasses at the same time. "I've been watching that thing for five minutes now. And do you know what I think it is, fellows?"

"What?" demanded Jack, who could not leave his duties even for the minute that it would take to glance through the glasses.

"A wreck!" exclaimed Josh, with thrilling emphasis.

Then everybody sat up, and began to look eagerly in the direction mentioned. It was far out over the troubled waters; and the object could only be seen when it happened to be lifted on the crest of a wave.

"It is that same, upon me worrd!" cried Jimmie, presently. "I cud say the thing thin as plain as the nose on me face."

"And boys, there's some kind of a flag floating on it," Josh went on.

"Upside down?" questioned Nick, eagerly.

"Looks like it to me," came the answer.

"Then it's a wreck, all right; because that's the signal of distress," Nick continued, now raising Herb's glasses for a look.

"Oh! my! I believe it's them!" he ejaculated a minute later.

At that Jack could stand it no longer.

"Here, Jimmie, you grab hold, and run this boat," he said. "Keep her nose pointed just as she runs now, and whatever you do, don't swing around, broadside on."

Then, as Jimmie took hold of the wheel, the skipper raised the glasses for a look, while George awaited his report with ill-concealed eagerness.

"There, look now, Jack!" cried Josh.

Presently Jack took down the glasses, and there was a grave expression on his face.

"What did you see, Jack?" demanded George. "Something that's bothered you some, I can tell by the way you frown."

"That's a sinking craft, all right, George," replied the other, as he turned on all the power his engine was capable of producing, and sent the Tramp speeding directly into the waves. "More than that, I'm afraid I did recognize it, and, just as Nick said, it's the power boat, Mermaid, carrying the banker, Mr. Roland Andrews, and his party. Boys, we must hurry to their rescue before they go down!"

CHAPTER XX

PAYING THE PENALTY

Immediately the little fleet of motor boats had taken up a course leading directly for the floating wreck. It looked like the height of folly for such miniature craft to thus put boldly out upon the bosom of that great inland sea; and nothing save a call to duty would ever have influenced Jack to make the venture.

They were strangely quiet as they continued to buffet the oncoming waves. Once in a while some one would ask the wielder of the marine glasses what he could see, and in this way all were kept informed.

Nick was trembling, so that there were times when he could hardly hold the glasses to his eyes.

"I see her!" he suddenly shouted in rapture. "Sallie's still there, fellows! I can tell her among the lot. There, she sees me, I think, for the darling is waving her handkerchief! She wants me to hurry along, fellows; perhaps the blessed waterlogged power boat is getting ready to dip under! Can't you throw on just a little more speed, Herb? Please do, to oblige me."

No one thought to laugh, nor did Josh come up true to his name just then; for somehow they seemed to understand that it was a grave matter, and no time for joking.

Jack could see the figures on the partly submerged boat with the naked eye now, they were getting so close.

"Do you see the other girl, Rita Andrews?" he asked Jimmie; and was more pleased than he cared to show when the Irish boy answered in the affirmative.

"Oh! I only hope we get there in time!" groaned Nick, as he fumbled at the cork life preserver, as though intending to put it on again.

"What are you going to do with that thing, Buster?" demanded Herb, sharply.

"Get it around me," the other replied, unblushingly.

"But you won't need it; there's not the least chance of our upsetting now."

"All the same," Nick responded, calmly; "how do I know but I may have to jump overboard after Sallie? She might slip in her great joy at seeing her preserver so near. And a pretty fellow I'd be not to keep myself ready to do the hero act. Besides, Herb, how do we know that the bally old boat mayn't take a notion to duck under, just when we get close by? I believe in being prepared."

"You're right, Buster," nodded the skipper. "Take my cork jacket too if so be you think you'll need it. But please don't go to jumping over just to show off. You might drown before her very eyes."

"Oh! I'll be careful, Herb. But since you say so, I believe I will keep your cork affair handy. She might need it; because you see, Sallie is no light weight, any more than me."

He crouched there waiting, doubtless counting the seconds as they passed, and anxiously taking note of all that went on in the quarter whence they were headed.

Jack himself grew more nervous the closer they drew to the wreck. He realized that those on board were in extreme peril; for the powerboat seemed to be gradually sinking lower, inch by inch. At almost any time now it might give one tremendous heave, and then plunge, bow first, down in many fathoms of water, perhaps dragging some of the people aboard to death.

But at the same time Jack was figuring just how he and Herb must approach the wreck on the leeward side, where it would in a measure protect the small motor boats from the sweep of the seas. Here they would be able to take aboard as many of the imperiled ones as the rescuing craft could reasonably hold.

Jack also noted that there was a large lifeboat on the sinking craft. Possibly the oars had been swept away, rendering the craft helpless and useless. But if it could only be launched, the crew might occupy this, and be towed to safety by one of the little motor boats.

He fashioned his hands into a megaphone, while Jimmie tended the engine for a minute, and in this way called out:

"Have that boat launched. It will hold the crew, and we will give them a tow to the shore. Quick, sir; you have no time to lose!"

He saw the captain of the powerboat, still wearing his uniform, though without the jaunty blue cap that had once been a part of his makeup, give hurried orders. Then the lifeboat was shoved off the low deck, being held with a rope.

And a few minutes later the Tramp and the Comfort hauled in close under the lee of the big powerboat.

"Ladies first!" sang out Nick, as he balanced himself so as to be able to render any needed assistance.

Greatly to his joy Sallie seemed to choose the Comfort as her refuge. Perhaps she recognized the fact that it was by all odds the largest of the three motor boats, and hence more suitable to her heft. But it would be hard to convince Nick that this was the true reason. She saw him, and was willing to entrust herself in the charge of one who bore himself so gallantly.

Jack meanwhile had the pleasure of assisting the pretty and vivacious little Miss Andrews, whose first name was Rita, into his boat; to be followed by another lady passenger, and then the banker himself. The balance of the passengers managed to embark on the Comfort. George stood by, and offered to take one or two; but no one seemed to particularly care to entrust themselves on such a wobbly craft.

The captain and his little crew entered the lifeboat.

"Now, everybody get away as quick as you can!" called the man in uniform, "because she's going down any minute. Make haste, or we may be drawn under by the suction."

George had taken the long rope attached to the bow of the lifeboat, and fastened it securely to a ringbolt at the stern of his Wireless. He now started away, as did the other rescuing craft.

And none too soon was this manœuvre accomplished. Hardly had they gone ten boat lengths before a little shriek from Sallie announced that the final catastrophe was about to take place.

There was an upheaval of the sinking powerboat, a tremendous surge, and then only bubbles and foam on the surface told where the unlucky pleasure craft had vanished.

Little Miss Andrews cried a bit, perhaps because of the nervous excitement; but her father cheered her up.

"Never mind, Rita," he said. "The boat was insured, and we can get another and better one when we want it. But for this season I think we've had about enough of the water. I tell you we ought to think ourselves fortunate to have these fine fellows come out to us just in the nick of time. We'll never forget it, will we, girlie?"

Whereupon Jack was delighted to see the tears give way to a bright smile, as Rita looked at him, and nodded.

"How queer it seems," she remarked demurely, a little later. "First Jack had to save my hat from a watery grave; and now he has rescued poor little me. Yes, I mean that he won't forget us, dad. And I hope that we'll see him some time at our Oak Park home, don't you?"

"We'll try and influence him, and also his brave chums, in whom I find myself deeply interested. Come to think of it, I fancy I already have something of an acquaintance with a Mr. Harvey Stormways, belonging in the town Jack calls his home. The one I met in Chicago was a banker, and a very clever gentleman."

"That is my father," said Jack, rosy with pleasure to think that his parent already knew Rita's father.

Later on they discovered a landing place and managed to get ashore. All of them were delighted to once more set foot on solid land after their recent harrowing experiences.

And such a night they made of it. The captain had wisely secured a lot of stores before leaving the wreck of the Mermaid, so that there was little danger of any famine. Besides, as George said, aside, any camp that had been able to withstand the raids and assaults of a Buster all this while, would not be caught without plenty of eatables in the larder.

Around the camp fire they even made merry, since no lives had been lost in the wreck. Mr. Andrews told how they had escaped the first storm, only to be caught in the second, and rammed by some floating object, the nature of which they could only guess.

The pumps were manned, but by slow degrees the water had gained on them in spite of all their herculean efforts. And as we have seen, only for the coming of the motor boat boys a tragedy might have followed.

In the morning Jack promised to take them out to the first steamer that could be signalled, the crew in the lifeboat being towed behind the Comfort.

This he did, assisted by Herb.

And the balance of the young cruisers stood on the wooded bank, waving their hats and cheering as long as they could make their voices heard.

Nick was as happy as any one had ever seen him. Sallie had seemed to be fairly smitten with the charms of the fat boy, or else fancied having some girlish fun out of the meeting and their one trait in common; for she certainly had hovered near Buster since breakfast time, "making goo goo eyes at him," as Josh declared. And now Nick, wishing to be in a position to see better than his chums, took the trouble to laboriously climb a tree that hung far out over the water.

Here, high above the heads of the rest, he sat and waved his red sweater, as an object that must attract the sparkling eyes of Miss Sallie longer than an ordinary hat, or white handkerchief.

"Hurray! hurray!" he shouted at the top of his voice; but perhaps Buster may have been too violent in his gestures, or else neglected to maintain his grasp on the limb; for suddenly there was an awful splash, and the fat boy vanished out of sight in the lake, which happened to be fairly deep close up to the shore.

CHAPTER XXI

ANOTHER SURPRISE

"Help! help!"

"What's all the row about?"

"Buster's fallen in again! Somebody get a rope, and lasso him!"

"There he comes up! My! what a floundering time! He may be drowned, Jack!"

But Jack knew better, and only laughed as he replied to Herb:

"You forget that he's still wearing that lovely cork life preserver. It gives him such a manly look; and Buster thinks it adds to the admiration of a certain young lady."

Meantime there was a tremendous lot of splashing going on in that little basin just under the big tree, where Nick had been perched at the time of his tumble.

Both arms were working overtime, like a couple of flails in a thrashing bee; while his chubby legs shot back and forth after the manner of an energetic frog. All the while Buster was spouting water like a miniature geyser; for his mouth had happened to be wide open at the time of his unexpected submersion.

"Throw me a rope, somebody!" he spluttered, as he continued to make manful efforts to keep from sinking. "What d'ye stand there gaping for? Can't you see I'm in danger of drowning? Hurry up your cakes, you sillies!"

There was no doubt but that Nick believed every word he spoke; for he was making a tremendous display of energy that would long remain a topic for wonder among his comrades.

Herb started to scurry around to find something that would be available in the rescue line.

"Jack, the poor fellow may be partly stunned, and unable to keep up much longer. Help me find a rope, won't you?" he cried, as he passed the other.

"Hold on, Herb, now watch how easy it is to save a drowning man," and as Jack said this he turned to where Nick was making a young Niagara Whirlpool Rapids of himself, and called sternly:

"Buster, stand up!"

Lo; and behold, when the imperiled fat boy proceeded to obey this command the water barely reached to his chest. Looking rather crest-fallen and sheepish he started to wade out of the lake; while the boys burst into a roar that must have even been heard by those on board the steamer.

Nick was in a rather pugnacious humor, for him, as he arrived dripping on the bank. Perhaps the merriment of his mates had something to do with it; but the chances are he dreaded lest a pair of laughing blue eyes on the departing steamer may have witnessed his ridiculous upset.

"Who pushed me in?" he demanded, as he gave vent to another upheaval of water. "Tell me that, will you? It was a mean trick, and he ought to be ducked just as bad as I was. Seems like a pity a fellow can't just sit up on the limb of a tree to wave good-bye to a pretty girl without some envious rival putting up a game on him. Who did it? I dare him to tell!"

"Rats! you're away off your base, Buster!" cried George.

"Quit raising the lake that way, can't you?" complained Josh. "Want to flood us out of our camp, do you?"

"Buster, nobody was near you when you fell," said Jack. "I don't think there was one of us within ten feet of the tree. And besides, you were up out of reach. You let go both hands and slipped. It was your own fault. And we didn't help you out because I knew you had on that cork thing; besides, the water wasn't over your head, as I found out some time ago. So don't accuse anybody of being mean."

"And next time you want to take the middle of the stage just let us know. You gave us an awful jolt," remarked George.

"Why, if I'd had heart disease I'd have dropped flat," vowed Josh.

"Oh! let up on me, can't you, and don't rub it in so hard?" grumbled the dripping Nick. "Now I've got to go and get these duds off. And it'll take a long while for 'em to dry. Nice way to use a new suit, ain't it?"

"Well, it's lucky for the trade that you've come up here." Herb put in. "The clothing business will take on a boom soon. What with Canada pussies, and upsets into the lake, you can get away with more suits than the rest of us."

"But I haven't got another bunch of clothes along," whimpered Nick, "and it's sure too chilly to run around without anything on. Jack won't you help me out?"

"I guess I can lend you a pair of trousers, Buster, if you can get into them. Don't forget that fine red sweater you possess. Josh, pull it down from that branch, will you? So you see, you'll get along till these duds dry out," replied the one addressed.

"But stick to the camp while you're wearing that sweater, Buster," warned Josh. "Perhaps there ain't any cows around here; but even a bull moose would want to boost you up in a tree if he ever saw that rag."

"Oh! I'll hug the fire, all right; don't you worry about me, Josh Purdue," was the fat boy's reply, as he made off, the water still oozing from his soaked garments in streams.

Jack wisely put in the balance of the morning fishing, and with abundant success, as was evidenced from the fact that they had another delightful fish dinner that noon, Josh serving the trout in his usual tempting manner, crisp and brown.

As his clothes had meantime dried, through the action of combined sun and camp fire, Nick gradually became himself again. It took considerable to upset his good nature; and the boys never could fully decide whether he had been in earnest concerning that episode of the "great splash," or simply pretending to be indignant.

"And now, what's the programme?" asked Jack, as, having eaten until they could no longer be tempted, they sat back to talk over the future activities of the motor boat club.

"Fellows," remarked George, seriously. "I've come to the conclusion that we're making a mistake in cruising over such big water as this."

"Hear! hear!" called Nick, clapping his hands.

"Boats as small as ours seem out of their element on an ocean," continued the skipper of the Wireless, steadily. "They're all right in such places as the Thousand Islands, where plenty of harbors are in sight all the time. But just think what might happen up here. Suppose the wind had chopped around the other night, instead of kindly holding off till morning. What would have happened to us?"

"Oh! well," remarked Herb; "we all know the answer to that riddle, George. Since we couldn't well make out into the open lake in the storm during darkness, why, every boat must have been smashed against the rocks. Makes me shiver to just think of it; and that's right, fellows."

"Perhaps one or more of us might have gone under." George went on. "Now, when we got permission to make this cruise we promised not to take unnecessary risks—am I right, fellows?"

"Sure you are, George. Hit up the pace, will you? Buster here is getting sleepy, waiting for the verdict," Josh said, after his customary fashion.

"Then I'm going to offer a suggestion; and if Jack says so, I'll put it in the form of a motion," George continued.

"Make it a motion without all this fuss and feathers," observed Herb.

"I move, then, that we abandon our original intention of knocking along this north shore of Superior till we arrive at Duluth, where we could ship our boats home. It wouldn't pay us for the trouble and the danger. It's a barren country. If we had an accident there's no place to have repairs done short of several hundred miles. In a word, fellows, this is no hunting ground for little motor boats. Besides," with a sly glance toward Nick, "what if our grub gives out, as it's likely to do at any time, once Buster gets to feeling himself again; why, we might starve to death, fellows, in the midst of plenty."

"You've heard the motion, fellows—that we change our programme, and give up this Lake Superior trip. All in favor say aye!" Jack remarked.

A chorus of assents followed.

"Contrary, no!" went on the commodore; but only silence followed.

"Motion is carried unanimously," Jack went on. "And now, let's consider what is to take the place of this trip. We've still got some weeks ahead of us, the fishing's fine, and we're a long way from Milwaukee. Somebody suggest something."

George and Jack had of course talked this thing over more than once recently. So no one was surprised when the former immediately jumped up, and began:

"For one, I'm of the opinion we couldn't do better than return over part of the way we came. Between the Soo and Mackinac Island there's fine cruising ground to be explored. We can take a different route part of the way back through the St. Mary's River, and perhaps find new mud banks, with a few more strange animals on the Canada side. Besides Jack says the bass fishing is just great in some places they told him about at the Soo."

"Hurrah! Me for the St. Mary's then," Nick shouted, to hide his confusion at mention of strange beasts, for of course he knew what that referred to.

"The prospect of the merry bass frizzling over the coals coaxes Buster," declared Josh; "but on general principles, fellows, I don't see how we could improve on that programme. Count me in on it, George."

"Any other suggestions?" asked Jack. "If there are, now is the time to speak up, before we decide our plans. We can settle on just the day we ought to leave Mackinac for the run down Michigan to Milwaukee, and so get home on the dot. How is it, fellows? Do I hear another scheme offered?"

"Make it unanimous, Jack," said Herb. "You know we're pretty much of one mind; and we ought to get all the fun going out of that programme."

"Then we start back tomorrow?" said Jack.

"Right after breakfast," Josh added.

"Good gracious!" exclaimed Nick. "I hope none of you would be silly enough to ever think of leaving here before breakfast!"

"Oh! that will never happen, so long as we have an alarm clock in the bunch. We depend on you, Buster, to warn us when it's time to eat our three meals a day," George said blandly.

"Now, I didn't expect that of you George," remarked Nick. "But if you really mean it, thank you! I'm glad to know I'm of some use to the crowd."

"Why, Buster, we wouldn't know how to keep house without you," remarked Jack.

"What would we be after doing with the leftovers?" ventured Jimmie.

"And how would I keep my big boat evenly balanced?" demanded Herb. "Sure you fill a place in the circle, Buster, and a very important one. We'd miss you if you ever gave up the ship, and took the train back home."

"Well, I promise you I won't," smiled Nick; "at least so long as you keep up the same sort of bill of fare we've had today. Yum! yum! what's the use of wasting a fine piece of browned trout like that? I call it a wicked shame. Here, Josh, don't you dare throw that away. Set it aside on that nice clean piece of birch bark. Somebody might get hungry later on, and enjoy a bite."

This standing joke of Nick's clamorous appetite seemed never to lose its edge. The rest of the boys could always enjoy seeing him make way with his share of the meal. In fact, had a change come over the fat boy, they would have felt anxious, believing him sick.

So Jack went back to his fishing, of which he seemed never to tire, and the others found something to employ their time and attention while the afternoon sun dropped lower toward the western horizon.

By now the Big Lake looked like a lookingglass, so still had the waves become. A haze prevented them from seeing any great distance away—one of those mid-summer atmospheric happenings that are apt to develop at any time when the weather is exceedingly warm.

Evening came at last, and they sat as usual around the camp fire, having enjoyed the meal Josh and his willing assistants, Jimmie and Nick, had placed before them. Everything looked favorable for getting off in the morning; and should the lake remain calm Jack believed they might be able to make the Soo by another night.

Suddenly, and without the slightest warning a disturbing factor was injected into this quiet restful camp. Jack thought he heard a sound like a groan near by, and raised his head to listen. Yes, there was certainly a movement at the west side of the camp, as though something was advancing. And as he stared, his hand unconsciously creeping out toward the faithful little Marlin shotgun, a figure arose and came staggering toward the group.

Loud cries broke out as the boys scrambled to their feet. And there was a good excuse for their consternation; for in this ragged, dirty, and altogether disreputable figure they recognized, not a wandering hobo, but Bully Joe, the crony of Clarence Macklin!

CHAPTER XXII

TO THE RESCUE

Joe Brinker was a sorry sight as he staggered forward, and fell almost at the feet of Jack. He certainly looked as though he had been through a rough experience since last they saw him with Clarence aboard the Flash.

"Why, it's Joe!" exclaimed Nick, as though he had just recognized the intruder.

Jack had jumped forward, and was now bending over the newcomer.

"Here, Josh, any hot coffee left in the pot?" he demanded, seeing that the other looked utterly exhausted, as though he might not have partaken of food for many hours.

Josh immediately poured out a cup, and handed it to Jack.

"Sit up here, and swallow this, Joe," said Jack, supporting the fellow with one arm, and holding the tin cup to his lips.

Joe eagerly gulped down the warm drink. It seemed to do him a world of good right on the spot; for when a cup of hot tea or coffee is available, it is utter folly to think strong drink is necessary in reviving a chilled or exhausted person.

"Oh! that tastes fine. Got any more, boys? I'm nearly starved," he exclaimed, almost crying with weakness.

Already had Nick hurried over, and seized upon several cold flapjacks that possibly he had placed away, against one of his little bites between meals. Surely Nick ought to know what an awful thing hunger was. One of the most dreadful recollections of his life was a time when he had been compelled to go all of eight hours without a solitary scrap of food passing his lips!

Soon Joe was devouring the flapjacks with the eagerness of a hungry dog, to the evident delight of Buster, who always found pleasure in seeing any one eat heartily.

"Now tell us what happened, Joe?" said Jack, after they had watched the other make away with the last scrap, and look around for more.

"Yes, don't you see we're just crazy to hear?" Josh exclaimed.

"Did you get caught in that storm?" demanded George, suspecting the truth.

Joe nodded his head in the affirmative, and they could see a shudder pass over his form, as though the remembrance was anything but cheerful.

"Then the Flash must have been wrecked?" George went on, horrified as the remembrance of Clarence's face came before him.

"Gone to flinders!" muttered Joe. "Smashed on the rocks, and not a scrap left to tell the story. Gee it was tough, all right!"

"W—was Clarence drowned?" Nick gasped, with awe-struck face; and quivering all over like a bowl full of jelly.

"Oh! no, neither of us went under," replied Joe, promptly, to the great relief of all the boys. "But we came mighty near it, I tell you, fellers. I'm a duck in the water, you know, and I guess I helped Clarence get ashore. He said I did, anyway. And there we was, far away from everything, with not one bite to eat, or even a gun to defend ourselves against wild animals."

"Wow! that was tough!" admitted Nick, sympathetically; as he remembered his own exploit when the Canada lynx invaded the camp, and how useful the shotgun proved on that occasion.

"But it wasn't the worst, fellers! There's more acomin'!" Joe went on, shaking his head solemnly.

"My gracious! did wild animals get poor old Clarence after all?" George asked.

"No," Joe went on, with set teeth, "but a couple of men did that was as bad as any wild animals you ever heard tell of. They found us trying to make a fire to dry our wringing wet clothes; and they just treated us shameful. See this black eye I got just because I dared answer back. They kicked poor Clarence like he was a bag of oats."

"Two men, you say?" Jack asked, frowning darkly. "What sort of men could they be to act like that toward a pair of shipwrecked boys?"

"They looked like lumber cruisers, or prospectors that never struck it rich," Joe continued. "They had a grouch agin everybody. First thing they took what money we had, and Clarence's fine watch that was water-soaked and wouldn't run. Then they found out who we was by reading some letters he carried. I saw 'em talking it over; and then they tied us to a couple of trees."

"Why, I never heard of such a wicked thing!" ejaculated the startled Nick; whose mouth kept wide open while he listened to this thrilling story of Joe's.

"Do you think they meant to try and force blackmail?" asked the far-seeing George, whose father was a lawyer, it may be remembered.

"They said something about him writing home for more money to buy another motor boat," Joe replied. "And Clarence said he never would do it, not even if they tortured him. But I'm afraid a few more kickings like they gave us will break down his spirit."

"Then you managed to escape?" Jack went on, wishing to learn the whole thing.

"Yes. I worked loose, and slipped away when neither of 'em was lookin'," answered the ragged and dirty figure. "But give me some more grub, fellers. I'm starving, I tell you. They refused to give us a bite to eat till Clarence agreed to do all they wanted of him. Anything, so's I can fill up. I've got a hole down there that feels like Mammoth Cave."

Again it was Nick who hastened to procure another stock of eatables, crackers and cheese, or anything else that came handy.

"When did you escape, Joe?" asked Jack, seriously as though some plan had already started to form in his active brain.

"Don't know for sure," replied the exhausted one. "Sometime after noon, though. They was layin' down and snoozing when I got free. I wanted to find a knife, and cut Clarence loose too; but the risk scared me. And Clarence, he told me to hurry and get off for help. You see, one of the men was sitting up, and rubbing his eyes; so I just sneaked away."

"Did they follow after you, Joc?" asked George.

"Never waited to see," replied the other, "but just cut stick, and hurried off. Oh! I've had an awful time getting along near the shore. Dassent get out of sight of the lake because you see I was that scared I'd get lost. I tumbled a thousand times, cut my head and hands on the rocks, nearly slipped into the lake twice, and was just ready to lay down and die, when night came on. Then I saw a fire over here, and just managed to make the riffle. Give you my word, fellers, if it'd been half a mile more I never'd got to camp."

"Then Clarence is still in the hands of those two rascals?" Jack asked.

"I reckon he is, 'less they saw fit to let him go free; and from what I seen of 'em, that ain't their game."

"How far do you suppose that place was away from here?" came from careful George.

Joe sat silent for a minute. He seemed to be trying to figure what manner of slow progress he may have made since effecting his freedom.

"I thought I'd gone nigh twenty miles, judgin' by the way I felt," he finally said; "but come to figger it out I reckon it mightn't abeen more'n five."

"Toward the west, you mean; for you came from that direction?" Jack continued.

"Yes, that's so, over that way," pointing as he spoke.

Jack turned to his chums.

"It's up to us, boys," he said soberly. "Clarence has never been one of us; but he belongs to our school. We'd never forgive ourselves if we went back to the Soo tomorrow, and left him in the hands of these scoundrels. Do you agree with me?"

"That's right, Jack!" sang out George.

"Sure we would be cold-blooded to think of it," Josh declared.

"Them's my sentiments," Herb spoke up; and both Nick and Jimmie nodded their heads violently, to prove that they were in no way behind their comrades in wishing to do a good deed toward one who had long been an open enemy.

"Then let's consider what way we ought to go about it," Jack proceeded, with an air of business. "It's out of the question for us to try and go back the way Joe came. We couldn't make it under hours; and from his looks none of us are hankering after the experience. But there is a way to get there quickly."

"The boats?" George put in.

"One boat ought to carry all who will go, and let that be the Comfort, with five of us on board, taking the two guns to make a good show," Jack proceeded.

Nick immediately set up a whine.

"I guess I have feelings," he declared. "Don't I know you're just going to shut me out of this rescue game? I'm ready to do my part as well as the next one, ain't I? What you want to leave me behind for?"

"You've got to obey orders, Buster," said George.

"And besides, with so many aboard, the bully old Comfort might founder," Josh thought it necessary to remark.

"Besides, you are going to have your share of the work, and along a line you always like," Jack went on; "for while we're gone, it shall be your duty to make a new brew of coffee, fill Joe here cram up with all he can eat, and have something ready for Clarence when we bring him back. So you see, Buster, your duty is as important as any of ours. Every one in their particular line. You can't fight as well as Jimmie here; but you do know how to provide against starvation."

Nick smiled broadly again, entirely appeased.

"Count on me, Commodore," he said, briskly. "Where's that coffeepot right now? I'll do my duty to the letter. Why, it's a pleasure to look after the wants of a hungry fellow. It gives me something of an appetite just to think of the work I've got cut out for me."

Jack put Nick and Joe out of his mind, after trying to get a little information from the latter, with regard to the character of the place where the Flash had been wrecked, and the two hard looking customers were supposed to be still stopping.

They went aboard the Comfort. Jack himself decided to run the boat, with the assistance of Herb and George. Above all things, silence was of more value to them just then than speed, if they hoped to steal up on the captors of Clarence without being detected.

"Good luck!" called Nick, as the broad beamed motor boat started quietly away.

CHAPTER XXIII

HOMEWARD BOUND

"Look! isn't that a fire over there?" asked sharp-eyed George, as he gripped Jack's arm suddenly.

They had been moving cautiously along for the better part of an hour, striving in every way possible to avoid any drumming sound, such as nearly always betrays the presence of a motor boat near by.

And in all that time they may have only covered some four miles, or possibly five; for no effort was made to drive the Comfort at even half speed.

"Looks like it," Jack replied, after a quick survey. "But how is it we didn't glimpse it before?"

"I think a point of rocks must stick out between, and we've just opened the pocket," George replied, in a whisper.

Of course Jack had immediately shut off the power, so that old reliable Comfort stopped her forward movement, lying there on the dark waters like a log; for not a light of any description did they carry aboard.

"Do we go ashore now?" asked Josh, softly; for all of them had been warned not to speak above a whisper from the time they started forth on their errand of mercy.

"Yes," Jack replied. "That's one reason we've been keeping so close in. I'll drop into the dinky, and use the paddle. Foot by foot I can pull the motor boat to shore, and then we'll land."

"How lucky there's not a breath of wind," Herb remarked, as he helped Jack draw the small tender alongside, and then crawl over the side.

Presently Jack was working away, having attached the painter of the boat to a cleat at the bow of the Comfort. His method of using the paddle insured utter silence. Had it been an expert hunter, moving up on a deer that was feeding on the lily pads along the border of a Canada stream, he could hardly have manipulated that little spruce blade with more care.

And so, foot by foot, the motor boat was coaxed in nearer the rock-bound shore. When Jack had finally succeeded in accomplishing his end he next sought some place where those still aboard could disembark, and the Comfort be tied up while they went about the business that had brought them there.

"Now, what next?" asked Herb, when the entire five had reached land, and the boat was amply secured to a split rock, with little danger of any injury resulting, because there was no wind and hence no movement to the water.

"We've got to advance," Jack replied. "So as to get around that point; when we'll see the camp Joe told us about. Those fellows have got a big rowboat, he said, but hate to work the oars. He said they first talked of making the boys do the rowing; and then that scheme for getting more money came up. Are you ready for the job?"

"I am that," said Jimmie, promptly, flourishing a club that looked like a baseball bat; and which would be apt to prove a formidable weapon in hands that were as clever as those of the stout Irish lad.

"Count me in," remarked Herb, who was carrying a hatchet; having nothing else to serve him as a threatening weapon that might strike terror to the hearts of the enemy.

"And I'm only too anxious to look in on 'em. Let me eat 'em up!" Josh growled, flourishing the camp bread knife in a most dreadful fashion.

George had his rifle, and of course Jack carried the repeating Marlin shotgun which had proven its value on many another occasion.

"Then come on, and be mighty careful, everybody," Jack cautioned, as he led off.

They remembered what Joe had said about the "rough sledding" he had found in his endeavor to keep close to the water's edge, so that he might not get lost. And every one of the five were willing to admit that Joe spoke the truth when he told this; for they made the slowest kind of progress.

Still, every yard passed over took them so much closer to the goal. And so long as they did not tumble and make a noise that would warn the enemy, it mattered little or nothing about the time they took in covering the ground.

After a long time spent in this sort of crawling business Jack believed he could see what seemed to be a fire flickering among the stunted trees.

Calling the attention of the others to this, he changed his course a bit, in order to find an easier route, and perhaps come upon the camp from behind.

For tenderfeet the five boys seemed to be making a pretty clever advance. They could now see a man stretched at full length near the fire, as if sleeping; though now and then a puff of smoke told that he was only taking it easy, and indulging in his pipe.

A little farther and they glimpsed the second fellow. He towered up like a house, being all of six foot-three, and bulky in proportion. But then, as Jack well knew, a man is only a man, no matter what his size, when he is looking into the muzzle of a rifle and modern repeating shotgun. And even this giant might well quail when brought to book.

The boys were now creeping through the bushes, and getting very close in. All the while Jack was eagerly trying to see what had become of Clarence. At first he could discover nothing of the other; and became chilled with a deadly fear that these cowards might have gone to extremes; though he could hardly bring himself to really believe it.

George was the first to find out what had been done with the prisoner.

"I see him," he whispered close to Jack's ear. "He's lying on the ground over by that stump of a tree."

Guided by these directions Jack was enabled to also place Clarence. There was certainly a figure lying there, and it must be the companion of Joe; for the latter had said there were only two of the scoundrels.

Jack bobbed his head back in a hurry, after he had made this little survey of the enemy's camp. For the big man had arisen to his feet, and started toward the very place where Clarence lay.

"Be ready!" muttered Jack, seeming to understand that the crisis must now be very close upon them.

Arriving at the spot, the giant bent over, and they could hear his growl as he spoke harshly:

"Made up yer mind yet, younker? Will ye write thet letter jest as we tell ye, and let a couple o' honest though unfortunit men have a square chanct to rake in a leetle pile? Speak up, now, d'ye hear?"

He accompanied his words by a brutal kick that gave Jack and George a spasm of anger.

"No! no! no!" shouted the obstinate Clarence, still undismayed; for his pluck was the best part of him, and had always been.

At that the big brute raised his heavy boot with ugly words. It was doubtless his full intention to dash it against the side of the helpless boy, regardless as to what the consequences might be. But he changed his mind.

"I wouldn't do that if I were you, mister!" said Jack, in an even, clear voice, as he and George suddenly stood up in full sight.

He had covered the giant with his gun, and George was ready to do the same for the man with the pipe the instant he bounded to his feet.

"Stand still, both of you, or we'll shoot!" George shouted.

This was a signal for the other three who were behind, and they suddenly made their appearance, waving their crude weapons menacingly.

The two men were apparently taken completely by surprise. They saw that the tables had been suddenly turned. And somehow, although these were only boys who confronted them, there was a grim air of business about those unwavering guns that neither of the cowards fancied at all.

Jack had not known what the result was going to be. He hardly anticipated that the men would dare attack them in the face of those weapons. And he had arranged with George that should they show signs of flight, no one was to raise a hand to prevent them.

When therefore the giant gave vent to a whoop and turning, galloped toward the water's edge, neither of the boys pulled trigger; though Josh let out a shout as though he might be chasing after; which he was not, all the same, for he did not fancy the looks of either of the rascals.

The second man took to his heels also, dodging to the right and left in a ridiculous manner, as if expecting every second to hear the crash of Jack's gun, and feel himself being peppered with bird shot.

They could be seen tumbling madly into their rowboat, and pushing out on the lake with all possible speed.

"Let 'em go!" said Josh, grandly, as he replaced his bread knife in the leather scabbard he had made for it, so as to avoid any chance of cutting his fingers by coming in contact with its keen edge, when rummaging in the locker aboard the Wireless, where the cooking things were kept.

Jack was already stooping over Clarence, and in a jiffy had severed the cords that bound him hand and foot.

"I'm awful glad you came, Jack!" said the other weakly. "I believe that coward would have killed me if I didn't give in to him."

"Here, work your arms and legs as fast as you can, Clarence!" said George. "We've got to get out of this in a hurry now, or they might even find the Comfort, and run away with her. You're going back with us, you know. Joe got in and told us."

The two men having put what they thought a safe distance between themselves and the boys, began to shout insulting remarks, and make the most terrible threats. Although they could not be seen out on the lake, it was not so difficult to know in what quarter they chanced to be at the time.

Angered by the insults, as well as the cruel manner in which they had treated Clarence and Joe, George picked up the shot gun which Jack had lain down for a minute, and before any one could stop him had discharged it.

That some of the many little lead pellets in that shell had stung the profane scoundrels in the rowboat, the boys understood from the howl that arose, followed by the splashing of oars, telling that they were pulling madly away before a second shot added to their troubles.

"Now come with us, Clarence," said Jack.

They did not have to be so careful making their way back to where they had left the steady going old Comfort. And once aboard, the return trip was quickly accomplished. In camp Clarence was soon given all the food and coffee he could manage; and he professed himself as very grateful for all the motor boat boys had done for him.

Since his speed boat had met with so tragic an end, Clarence declared that he had had enough of cruising, and would start straight home as soon as they reached the Soo, if the boys would lend them enough money to buy tickets—which programme he and Joe carried out; nor were our six friends at all sorry to see them vanish from view.

Leaving the Soo, Jack and his chums spent almost two weeks upon the crooked St. Mary's river, camping, fishing and enjoying themselves to the utmost. But never did they touch on Canadian soil but that poor Buster seemed to be dreadfully uneasy, sticking close to the fire, and breathing a sigh of genuine relief when once more afloat, with no unpleasant reminders wafted after them.

Jack and Nick had made up a little programme for themselves, which they sprung upon their comrades later, when leaving the three boats at Milwaukee to be sent by rail to the home town on the Upper Mississippi.

This was nothing more nor less than saying good-bye to the rest of the boys in Milwaukee, and taking a little run down to Chicago, "to see the sights, you know," as Nick cleverly put it. But everybody guessed that the greatest attraction which all Chicago could boast for the deserters would be found within the borders of Oak Park, and under the roof of the banker, Mr. Roland Andrews.

And so the great cruise had finally come to an end. Looking back the boys found no reason to regret their course. True, there might be a number of incidents that would stand out for a long time with a bit of harshness; but time mellows all such things; and even Buster would laugh just as heartily as any of his chums when his adventure with the bull, or the pretty Canada pussy-cat, were mentioned.

They had had such a glorious time of it that undoubtedly other trips must be talked over during the coming winter; and with the coming of the holiday season once again the motor boat boys would be found ready to set out again on their search for new adventures.

Jocko went home with George and was a source of considerable costly amusement in the Rollins' home.

We shall surely hope and expect to continue the pleasant acquaintance formed in the pages of the several books already published; and in new fields accompany Jack Stormways and his chums, with their gallant little boats, through other scenes, where true American pluck and endurance, such as they have always shown, must carry them through all perils to success.

THE END

9 781836 573289